Death of a Marseilles Man

From my seat in one of the cars on the scenic railway I look down on the milling crowd. Up. Down. Up. Down. The rush of the wind on my face . . . Then, on the back of my neck, the breath of the man who has grabbed hold of me. I struggle. A blow on the head. Another. Everything starts to circle and sway . . .

Paris, May 1957 'Lots of fun in the Place de la Nation!' screamed the poster in the restaurant window. And at that moment in time Nestor Burma, fearless chief of the Fiat Lux Detective Agency, needed some entertainment.

But fighting for his life 100 feet up on a scenic railway was a little more excitement than he'd bargained for. His attacker, Roger Lancelin, now lies dead under the metal scaffolding of the track. Why should this seemingly ordinary commercial traveller from Marseilles want to kill him? And who was the beautiful stranger in the blue dress, their fellow passenger on the train?

At first Nestor believes he has merely been mistaken for an undercover policeman. Until he uncovers one very disturbing fact – almost a year ago to the day young Geneviève Lissert had been brutally thrown from the same train.

As the mystery runs deeper and deeper, Nestor follows an ancient trail of murder and greed down the backstreets of the 12th . . .

Death of a Marseilles Man

Léo Malet

Translated from the French by Barbara Bray
General editor: Barbara Bray

MACMILLAN

First published in France in 1957 by Robert Laffont, Paris, as
Cassepipe à La Nation in the series *Les Nouvelles Mystères de Paris*

Also published in France 1983 by Editions Fleuve Noir

First published in the United Kingdom 1995 by Macmillan
an imprint of Macmillan General Books
25 Eccleston Place, London SW1W 9NF
and Basingstoke

Associated companies throughout the world

ISBN 0 333 64951 6

Copyright © Léo Malet 1957

This translation © Aramos 1995

The right of Léo Malet to be identified as the
author of this work has been asserted by him in accordance
with the Copyright, Designs and Patents Act 1988.

9 8 7 6 5 4 3 2 1

A CIP catalogue record for this book is available from
the British Library

Printed and bound in Great Britain by
Mackays of Chatham plc, Chatham, Kent

Contents

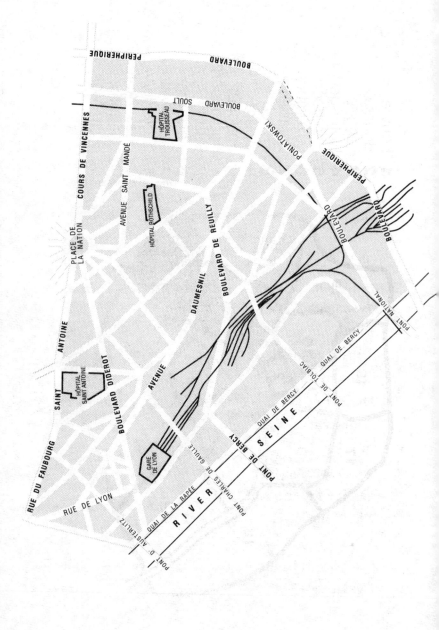

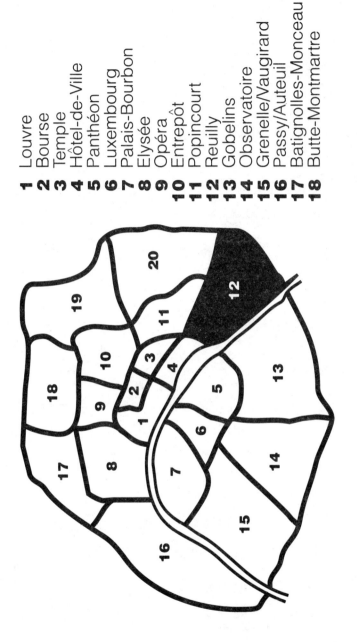

1 Louvre
2 Bourse
3 Temple
4 Hôtel-de-Ville
5 Panthéon
6 Luxembourg
7 Palais-Bourbon
8 Elysée
9 Opéra
10 Entrepôt
11 Popincourt
12 Reuilly
13 Gobelins
14 Observatoire
15 Grenelle/Vaugirard
16 Passy/Auteuil
17 Batignolles-Monceau
18 Butte-Montmartre

1 The Gare de Lyon

May, early May, and all day Paris had been treated to sunshine and showers alternately. Sometimes both together. Now I'd counted up twenty minutes without any rain. It couldn't last. It didn't.

As I drove by the column at the Bastille, heading for the rue de Lyon, the skies opened up again. Drops started to hit the windscreen and trickle down the glass, and I could hear others pattering on the roof. I switched on the wipers and joined in with their whingeing: 'It's raining, it's pouring, The old man's snoring . . .'

High up through the drizzle I could see the station clock, a great eye reproaching latecomers. But I wasn't late. The huge steel hands said five-forty, those on my watch said twenty to six, and the train I was interested in wasn't due till 18.05.

I found a place to park in the rue Abel (*absit omen*, as we autodidacts say) then sat in the car for a while waiting for the rain to stop. As it showed no signs of slackening, I put on the raincoat that had been lying crumpled up on the back seat, and made a dash for it. By the time I'd crossed the boulevard and run up the ramp into the station, the creases in my mac had all been washed right out.

I bought a ticket at a machine and went through a turnstile into the waiting area. The little bit of cardboard brought back memories I didn't care to dwell on, and I was still more put out when the first person I saw, standing by a bookstall, was a man of about my own age and size, wearing the same sort of raincoat as mine and an expression that wouldn't have looked out of place on an iceberg.

Grégoire. A cop. One of those who worked for my pal, Superintendent Florimond Faroux of the Paris CID.

I wished now that I'd gone into a bar to kill the quarter of an hour before the Cannes train was due. I was about to make a quick getaway when Grégoire spotted me, and before I knew it we were shaking hands.

'How's tricks?'

'Fine!'

He glanced at the platform ticket I still had in my hand.

'Going away?'

He was referring to the well-known fact that in my youth I'd often contributed to the railway's annual deficit by travelling free, gratis and for nothing.

Ignoring his grin, I explained I was there to meet Hélène, my secretary, who'd gone to acquire a sun-tan on the Côte d'Azur. He returned the compliment: he was there to meet his wife – she'd been to Marseilles to fetch his niece to stay with them for a few months.

He lit a home-made cigarette that smelled so awful

it blotted out the fragrance issuing from a locomotive fretting at a nearby platform. I got out my pipe to even things up.

He maundered on about Marseilles and the damage the Germans had done to it. People started blaming the Germans for everything once they'd lost the war. I answered in monosyllables. If any passers-by had overheard our exchanges they'd have taken us for two prize dimwits. When the conversation finally expired I didn't even try to revive it.

Then the approach of the train bearing my Hélène and Grégoire's family party back to Paris was announced over the loudspeaker, and the waiting throng all made for the main-line barrier. You'd never have thought this was an everyday occurrence. As Grégoire stood staring grimly along the rails with his hands in his pockets, for all the world as if he was waiting to nab Public Enemy No. 1, it struck me that with our similar coats and hats and not dissimilar figures we looked like a typical pair of plain-clothes cops. Hélène was sure to rib me when she saw us . . .

More crackling from the loudspeaker roused me from my reverie: the arrival of the 18.05 was imminent. But what drew in was only an electric train, without the poetry, the roaring and the smoke, of a steam-engine.

The passengers began to get out, and a whole cross-section of the human race was soon streaming by us. Some were natives of the South, burned brown by the sun. Some were palefaces. Some had suitcases. Some had no luggage at all. Some were slinky, elegant young women, the kind you never see except on trains or in railway stations, creatures whose mystery and charm derive from your knowing you'll never set eyes on them again. There were sun-tanned girls who'd obviously been living it up in smart hotels, and wan-faced girls who looked as if they were up from the provinces to go into service – but who six months from now would probably be on the street. There were serious faces, scanning the waiting crowd anxiously, then lighting up when they saw the person they sought. Cheerful faces. Tired faces. Close-shaven faces. Faces covered in stubble. Families. Couples. And people who were alone – alone where they came from, alone on their journey, and alone at their destination. Past the greetings, kisses and smiles of the rest these solitaries stalked contemptuously ahead into an inaccessible world of their own.

This was all very fine, but where was my Hélène? And if it was any consolation, Grégoire's luck didn't seem any better than my own.

By now there were no more passengers left on the train, and the porters were going along the platform slamming the doors. Just one batch of laggards still sauntered towards the exit, but the group didn't contain anything resembling a pretty girl.

Suddenly Grégoire let out a grunt of relief and hurried over to a woman escorting a female beanpole of about sixteen. They climbed all over one another for a few minutes, then Grégoire led them up to me, about to perform the usual introductions.

'But what about your secretary?' he said. 'Hasn't she come?'

'No hiding anything from the law, is there?'

'Must have missed the train.'

'No doubt. I'll go and find out the time of the next one.'

I extricated myself as politely as I could, consulted the arrivals board, then left the station, fed up with Grégoire for being such a bore and with Hélène for standing me up.

Anything for a moment's distraction: I went and joined a trio of North African loafers looking down into the Passage Moulin at the streetwalkers plying their trade outside the sleazy hotels. This had been the Chinese quarter until a few years before, but now it looked as if the Orientals were being ousted by the Algerians.

The spectacle soon palled, so I went and had an apéritif on the terrace of the Café des Cadrans. It had stopped raining, for a wonder . . .

Dinner time. I had dinner while I waited for the next train from Marseilles. But again Hélène wasn't on it.

Moral: Don't ever let them go the South of France on their own.

2 Dirty Work on the Scenic Railway

Hélène obviously wasn't going to turn up that day. I went back to the café for a liqueur, fetched the car from the rue Abel, and started to drive around aimlessly. I didn't feel like going to bed, I didn't feel like not going to bed; I didn't know what I *did* want. Then I caught sight of a poster in a restaurant window: 'The traditional Foire du Trône! Lots of fun in the Place de la Nation! Come to the Fair!' I went.

At least they'd made an effort. The entrance to the square was got up like the gates of a medieval town with massive grey walls on either side. There was a strong smell of sawdust and wet paint. A record player, hitherto silent, greeted my arrival with an ear-splitting howl, competing with the earth-shaking rhythms of the roundabouts. My nostrils were assailed by a mixture of diesel oil, fried potatoes, doughnuts, marshmallow, dust and the cheap scent favoured by skivvies on the spree and their escorts. Inspector Grégoire's cigarette was Chanel No. 5 in comparison. It wasn't hot enough for sweat. Pity. I mingled with the crowd.

Wrestlers, shooting galleries, dodgem cars, tombolas, fortune-tellers, makers of horoscopes. Swings of various kinds. A dwarf with two heads, a boy giant. Emma and her snakes. Eve and her daughters. Adults only. Medical curiosities. Judging by the sound of his voice, somebody somewhere must have been treading on Gilbert Bécaud's toes. More wrestlers. On my right, Kid Batignol, the Australian champion. On my left, X, the 'amateur' who has been acting as his stooge for the last ten years. Shrieks, whistles, laughter, tears. Candyfloss. Test your skill. Try your luck. Rows of clay pipes shot to smithereens. Pyramids of old tin cans collapsing. Ghost Train. Giant Wheel. Tableaux vivants fit to raise the dead. Bearded Lady. Performing animals. Loch Ness Monster. This way for the fire-eaters: a male and female savage from the ends of the earth, who will handle red-hot irons and swallow burning petrol with every appearance of pleasure on their primitive mugs. Step right in to enjoy this instructive spectacle . . .

From my seat in one of the cars on the scenic railway I look down on the milling crowd; on the trees lining the square; on Philippe Auguste and St. Louis on their columns. Up. Down. Up. Down. The rush of the wind on my face . . .

Then, on the back of my neck, the breath of the man who has grabbed hold of me. I struggle. A blow on the head. Another. Everything starts to circle and sway. Shout, shout, shout! I fall. And swirling all around me the trees, the buildings, the metal supports of the switch-back which I seem to knock against as I fall. Then everything gets slower and slower, slower and slower: perhaps this is what it's like when you die.

One last spasm, and I sink into a kind of dense fog. Then nothing.

From the depths of time, through endless layers of hazy thoughts, across the whole expanse of the Foire du Trône – voices.

'See to the girl!'

That's right. Women and children first.

'How is she?'

'Not moving.'

'And the bloke?'

I hear a faint little voice. Mine.

'Dead,' it says.

A volley of the sort of oaths I indulge in myself when I've got the strength.

I take a deep breath, a lungful of petrol fumes and the smell of burnt fat, and make the only movement I can. I open my eyes.

I'm sprawling on my seat in the car of the scenic railway, back now beside what they call the landing stage. I sense the presence of a crowd beyond the navy-blue uniform, black belt and leather holster that obstruct my view: the back view of a cop.

'See to the girl,' someone says again.

'Lift her out,' orders someone else.

She's in the car just in front of mine, lying back in the seat unconscious and white as a sheet. Her thick brown hair brushes against my knees. Three men, one of them in a white overall, lift her out without ceremony, disarranging her blue dress and revealing a pair of shapely legs encased in elegant stockings. I'd noticed the shapely legs when she got off the Loch Ness Monster. I'd also noticed she was alone, and as I too

was alone, I'd followed her. I didn't speak to her –
perhaps I only wanted to admire her pins. When she
decided to take a ride on the scenic railway, I got into
the seat behind her. And then . . .

The black belt made a U-turn, the holster moved
from right to left. The policeman bent over and seized
me by the shoulder.

'Hey!' he barked.

'Yes?'

'What's been going on?'

'I'll try to tell you if—'

'Come on out of there!'

He helped me stand up, and the blood rushed to my
head. As I stepped out on to the landing-stage I saw
the curious crowd through a reddish mist.

'Oh well, it wasn't the first time,' I muttered.

'What?' said the cop.

'Nothing.'

He suddenly let go of me, and I'd have fallen down
if one of the fairground staff hadn't caught me in time.
The cop had bent down to rummage in the wooden
compartment, in the place where my feet had been.
When he straightened up he had something in his hand,
and in his eye the sort of gleam that anticipates
promotion.

He stuck the object in front of me.

'What's this?'

'Can't you see? It's a gun.'

'A gun!'

I wasn't encountering the brightest of the boys in
blue today.

'Yes – mine. I gave the other bloke a bang on the

head with it to make him let go, and then I must have dropped it when I passed out.'

'Why did you pass out?'

'I was scared. I don't claim to be braver than the next man.'

'Never mind about that. All I'm concerned with is *this!*' – tapping the gun. 'I think we'd better have a little talk at the station.'

I handed him my papers and, as he checked laboriously through them, sat down on a stool kindly provided by the management.

'Right . . . Name?'

'Nestor Burma.'

'Profession?'

'Private eye.'

He sniffed disapprovingly and corrected me.

'Private detective . . . I see you've got a permit for the gun.'

'Yes. And let me tell you something you *won't* find in my papers. Superintendent Florimund Faroux is a good friend of mine.'

His eyes flashed. A reflection from a lamp, or wounded dignity?

'Are you trying to influence me, by any chance?'

I heaved a sigh that would have melted the heart of a prison warder.

'No need to be touchy!'

'That'll do. You may have had a shock, but whether or not you know the top brass at the Quai des Orfèvres is neither here nor there. I'm not here to argue the toss with you – I just want to hear your account of what happened.'

'By all means.'

'You can have your papers back, but I'll hold on to the gun for the present.'

I pocketed the first. He pocketed the second.

'Well?' he said.

'There isn't much to tell. I was just following a girl . . . the girl in the blue dress . . . What happened to her, by the way?'

'She fainted.'

'Scared at seeing us fighting, I suppose?'

It was understandable.

'Yes.'

'Good – I was afraid it might be more serious.'

'No – she just passed out. You were following her, you say? Why?'

'She had pretty legs.'

He looked incredulous. I went on. 'She bought a ticket for the scenic railway, and I got on behind her. A man got on behind me too, but I didn't pay any attention. The train started off, we whizzed down a slope, and our compartment was just negotiating a corner when I felt the bloke behind me grab me round the chest as if I were Brigitte Bardot. At first I thought he might have fallen for me, then that he'd been taken ill, but I soon realized he was trying to throw me overboard. There was a struggle. Some people down below must have noticed and called the police. The man hit me on the head with something or other but he didn't knock me out, so I got out my gun and hit *him* with the butt. I had no choice. And so he was the one who bought it. Flew out of the train like a bird. But as I said just now, it wasn't the first time. I'm used to it.'

'Used to throwing people down a hundred feet?'

'No – to getting knocked on the head and having a narrow squeak. And I was all right so long as I was just fighting to save my skin . . . It was afterwards it hit me. The reaction . . . That was why I passed out . . .'

'And no wonder,' said one of my cop's colleagues.

'No,' said another.

'And what about the bloke?' said my cop.

'What about him?'

'Were you following him too?'

'I was not! I don't even know what he looked like. There wasn't enough light for me to see him while we were struggling with one another . . . But I dare say his looks match his morals.'

'He's certainly no oil-painting now.'

'I suppose not. Dead, is he?'

'Yes.'

'H'm . . . Is he still lying where he fell?'

'Yes.'

'Could I see him?'

'I don't see why not.'

I got to my feet. I still felt horribly tired, but not so shaken up as before.

'So,' said the cop, 'you weren't following him, eh?'

'No. Why should I have been?'

'I thought you were a private detective.'

I didn't answer. If he wanted to try to think, let him.

3 Suspicions

The body lay underneath the metal scaffolding that supported the scenic railway, not far from an illuminated fountain which went on playing, tireless and indifferent. A crowd pressed up against the wooden barrier that fenced off the network of steel struts. Beyond the crowd the fun of the fair continued, but less stridently now because it was after ten o'clock, when Paris's anti-noise ban comes into force.

Someone had thrown a sheet over the corpse, and two policemen were mounting guard over it. My own cop twitched the sheet back with a theatrical gesture, as if he expected some significant reaction on my part. The crowd stirred.

Before turning into that broken doll the figure on the ground had been a well-built man of about forty. He was quite smartly dressed in a grey suit and a black and grey tweed overcoat. His shoes were of good quality. But in his fall he must have hit a girder, and the impact with the ground had done the rest: there wasn't much left of his face. There was enough, though, to confirm my previous impression that I didn't know my assailant from Adam. One of his hands rested on his stomach, as if he was anxious about some possible, but now very improbable, trouble from his appendix. The hand was well groomed and sun-tanned, and on one finger there was a signet ring. But none of this told me why the rascal should have tried to pitch me off the scenic railway.

At this point Inspector Garbois of the 12th Arrondissement, accompanied by another cop in plain clothes, came on the scene and took over. What Garbois lacked in stature he made up for by the size of his nose. When he blew it he must have felt as if he was shaking hands with a friend.

He asked my cop what had happened, gave both me and the corpse a piercing look, told me to give my version of the story, and asked me for my papers. Then:

'Nasty business, eh?'

I didn't disagree.

He rubbed his hands, as if that was the sort of business he liked.

'Have you searched the corpse?' he asked my cop.

'Yes, inspector.'

'Papers?'

They were handed over, read, and stowed away with mine.

'I'll take the gun too.'

He meant mine.

'What about the woman?'

'Taken to hospital, inspector.'

'Right. I'll leave you to see to the removal of the body, officer, and we'll be on our way.'

Which meant nearly everyone was off to the police station in the rue du Rendez-Vous: most of the cops, a member of the fairground staff as a witness, and yours truly. The only thing they left behind was the scenic railway itself. That was too big to move.

Hell's teeth! If that confounded little slut of a Hélène had turned up at the blasted station when she was supposed to, I'd be having a whisky with her now, listening to an account of her vacation and inspecting her sun-tanned cleavage . . . Instead of which, not only had I damn nearly been bumped off by a complete stranger, but for good measure I was being haled along the avenue du Trône in a bloody police van.

It was almost enough to make you use bad language.

When we got to the station and the people there asked what had happened, one of my escorts said somebody had fallen off the scenic railway.

'What? Again?'

'What do you mean – "again"?'

'The same thing happened last year. Don't you remember? A girl—'

'Oh yes, I remember now. But last year it was an accident. And the girl didn't die – she was only injured. But this time a couple of men had a fight, and one of them fell and was killed outright.'

The speaker pointed at me. As I wasn't the corpse, I could only be the person who'd tossed the other one down. Necks were craned.

Garbois led his party into the local superintendent's office, where for the umpteenth time I had to tell my story and answer questions. So did the witness. In the end they said we could go, but to make quite sure they realized who they were dealing with, I asked to be allowed to phone my friend Florimond Faroux, head of the CID. The local chief obligingly put through the call himself.

'Superintendent Faroux is on his way,' he said as he hung up. 'He isn't surprised something's happened to you. Apparently it's a frequent occurrence.'

So I sat on a bench and waited, smoking a pipe and watching a game of cards out of the corner of my eye. A drunk started to swear and curse in the cells; the heftiest of the uniformed cops went and out-cursed him. From the way the characteristic smell of the place was growing more and more pungent, I guessed it must be raining again outside.

The door finally opened to admit Faroux. I hurried over.

'Don't ask me what happened! I'll tell you!' I said as we shook hands.

He pushed me aside, saluted his colleagues, and went into a huddle with them.

Then he returned to me, pushed his hat back, and said: 'Let's have it, then.'

I remembered I'd lost my own hat in the struggle. I told him the story.

'Right,' said Faroux to the local chief. 'I'll answer for our friend here. No need to keep him any longer. But to get back to the business in hand – do we know who the victim was?'

The local chief showed him the papers Garbois had taken from the body.

'His name was Roger Lancelin,' he said. 'Born in Meaux in 1918. Commercial traveller. Lived in Marseilles, according to this identity card, though it looks a bit dubious to me . . .'

Faroux picked up the card and agreed.

'There's quite a lot of money in his wallet, but nothing else. Not a single letter or envelope, not even a business card. And nothing to show where he was staying in Paris. Rather peculiar, eh?'

Faroux nodded. 'And what about the woman? The one who fainted?'

The other consulted a slip of paper.

'Simone Blanchet, twenty-five years old, single, lives in the rue de la Brèche-aux-Loups. They took her to the Hôpital Rothschild for observation. Apparently she's still shaken, but one of our men has interviewed her. She didn't say much, except that she'll never set foot in a fairground again. She saw the two men fighting, but doesn't know which of them started it. She says she was on her own and didn't know anyone else there.'

'Were you thinking she knew at least one of the two men?'

'Well . . . it doesn't cost anything to wonder. But I suppose we were wrong both about her and about your friend. It was his occupation that made us suspicious.'

'Yes,' laughed Faroux. 'I suppose the licence of a private eye is as good as a criminal record any day! Well, come along, Burma. I've got a car waiting outside.'

'I left mine near the fair,' I said. 'Will you drop me off?'

I recovered my papers and the gun, and followed Faroux out to the car. I was right. It was raining again.

'How are things? Plenty of work?' said Faroux, settling back as we drove along.

'Nothing at the moment,' I answered. 'And I didn't know Lancelin, and I wasn't following him, if that's what you were thinking.'

'A nasty business, though.'

'That's what everyone says. And for once I agree.'

'Of course, we make a lot of enemies in our profession, you and I . . . Maybe—'

'I thought of that, but it won't work. I had a good look at the chap, and I'd never seen him before in my life. And after all, it may not be such a shady affair as all that – perhaps he was just off his head. And maybe he wasn't the only one – I heard someone at the station say a girl fell off the scenic railway last year . . .'

'And you think he was the one who pushed her?'

'I didn't say that! I was thinking of a crazy Hungarian I read about, who got such a thrill out of seeing a railway crash that he proceeded to arrange a few for himself. Perhaps our chap witnessed the girl's accident a year ago, enjoyed the sensation, knew he couldn't expect it to happen again very often, so decided to set up a repeat performance on his own account . . .'

Faroux gave me a pitying look. 'Where did you say your car was?'

I looked out into the darkness. We were approaching the avenue de Bel-Air.

'This'll do, thanks – it's just around the corner.'

The driver pulled up. I got out and shook hands with Faroux through the window.

'When are things going to stop happening to you, Burma?' he said. 'You've only got to put your nose out of doors and . . . Hell, why don't you just stay at home? Spend your evenings with some nice dame, Hélène for instance, or maybe some friend's girl . . . ?'

'Oh? And what if the friend gets jealous?'

Faroux's car receded into the darkness, and I got into mine and lit my pipe. The sight of the smoke, lit up by the street lamps, helped me to think. It hung in a cloud for a moment, then drifted out through the window, writhing about like a flapper who's seen too many films. Everything was quiet now. Quieter than three hours ago. Through the rain-spattered windscreen I could see in the distance the booths and roundabouts of the Fair, swathed in tarpaulins for the night. A few lights showed here and there in the windows of the comfortable mobile homes that have replaced the picturesque old caravans. Behind the check curtains, amid the doll's-house furniture, they must all be talking about the evening's strange events. Always supposing they cared.

I cared, anyway. I sat and pondered, finishing one pipe and lighting another before I started the car up and headed for home and bed.

Though it didn't really get me very far, I now had some idea of the sort of misunderstanding that had made someone try to push me off the scenic railway.

4 Hypotheses

The next morning at nine I was awakened by the clamour of the telephone. Hélène, calling from Cannes to tell me her troubles. Apparently she'd tried to reach me yesterday, but couldn't get any answer. What had happened was that, hurrying to catch the train, she'd tripped and twisted her ankle, so she'd have to stay on down there for a few more days.

'Very well – but I'd have you know you and your sprain were nearly the death of me!'

'What? How come?'

'Look in today's papers for the details . . . Well, goodbye for now – be sure to get your golden-haired gigolo to massage your ankle!'

'His hair's black, actually,' she snapped, and hung up.

The phone rang again. Marc Covet this time. The reporter and soak who works on *Le Crépuscule*. 'Hi, Burma! I gather they tried to bump you off at La Nation!'

'How do you know?'

'I've got a few lines here by our cub reporter. But

I'd like more details, please, to work up for the midday edition. Were you there on business?'

'No! I just happened to come across a madman. Could you read me what you've got?'

I listened. It seemed accurate enough.

'Would you like me to add any comments?' said Marc, who loves to complicate things.

'No, thanks. It'll do as it is.'

We both hung up. I had a little gargle from the bottle I keep handy for the purpose, and started shaving. I was just drying my chin when I heard a ring at the door.

Florimond and Grégoire, like two genies out of a bottle. The first looked bored, the second self-important.

'Good morning,' said the superintendent. 'Here we are again. Shall we ever get you off our backs? . . . I think you know Grégoire?'

'We chatted for twenty minutes or so at the Gare de Lyon yesterday evening, around six o'clock. He was there to meet some relatives.'

'And you?'

'Hasn't he told you? Hélène was supposed to be coming back from a holiday on the Côte d'Azur by the same train as his wife and niece. But she didn't turn up. Missed the train.'

'Very annoying,' said Faroux.

'You're telling me.'

'Yeah . . . Do you know what Grégoire thinks? He thinks you were waiting for somebody else from Marseilles. Somebody who didn't come up to you because he saw you with someone else. But you joined up later in the evening at the Foire du Trône.'

I shrugged. 'This new generation of cops . . . Too keen for their own good . . .'

'Grégoire thought your attitude was rather odd at the station yesterday.'

'Oh, did he? Well, that was because of my platform ticket – it brought back awkward memories, especially in the presence of the law. I might well have looked a bit strained.'

'You looked very uncomfortable!' said Grégoire.

'I was. Recall some of your conversation if you want to know why.'

'I was being dim on purpose,' protested Grégoire. But with a blush.

'That'll do,' said Faroux. 'Who *were* you waiting for, Burma – Hélène or . . . Lancelin?'

'Hélène.'

I opened a drawer. 'Look – here are the postcards she sent me from the Côte. Here's the letter saying when she'd get back. She rang just now to tell me she'd sprained her ankle and had to stay on for a few days . . . You can check with the post office if you like.'

'Right,' said Faroux, handing the correspondence back. 'Perhaps Grégoire did jump to conclusions. Don't hold it against him.'

'It's his job. You all do it. According to his papers, Lancelin lived in Marseilles – OK. But that doesn't mean he came up to Paris yesterday, and by that particular train – he might have been living here for some time. Have you got any recent information?'

They hadn't and, with apologies for their suspicions, they left. I wasn't sure if I'd convinced them, though: there's nothing more difficult to put across than the truth. So I was still likely to have the two of them yapping at my heels, especially Grégoire. I couldn't help laughing. He hadn't been all that wide of the mark. I'd have liked to see their faces if I'd told them everything!

'Listen, my friends. I really was waiting for Hélène, but with Grégoire and me standing there together wearing the same sort of hat and raincoat, and him scrutinizing everybody like a lynx – we stood out from the crowd like a couple of sore thumbs! As cops! So as you've got such ready imaginations, imagine Lancelin *was* on that train, that he had reason to be good at spotting plain-clothes men, and that he assumed we were there on his account. Later on he goes to the Fair, for some special reason or just to pass the time, like me; he sees me there and thinks I'm following him. As a matter of fact I had the same feeling myself once or twice – as if I was being spied on as I wandered round the sideshows. Anyhow, when he sees me get on the switchback he gets on behind me and tries to heave me out . . . He must have had his reasons. Don't you think it would be interesting to know what he'd come to Paris *for*? You'll probably get around to finding out in due course – but I'm going to try to beat you to it.'

It was just after midday when I got to Marc Covet's office at the *Crépuscule*.

'Was the article all right?' said Marc, nodding at the paper in my hand.

'Fine. You cracked me up nicely. That should bring the Agency some customers . . . But what I'm really here for is to ask if you've got a photograph of Lancelin, either from the police or from some other source.'

'Only some that a reporter who works for me managed to take at the morgue. But they're not fit to be shown around.'

He was right. They were very unappetizing. But I had an idea.

'Haven't you got someone on the staff who could touch them up and make them more presentable? They won't be an exact likeness, but they'll be better than nothing.'

Marc fixed that up for about four in the afternoon, and we went out for some lunch. Afterwards, while he went out to Montrouge on a story, I made for the *Crépu*'s archives, where I sent for the file covering the first quarter of 1956. Half-choked with the aroma of mouldy paper and printer's ink, I plunged into my researches.

Ah! Got it. Eighth of May 1956.

'Strange accident at the Foire du Trône. Young woman falls from scenic railway.

'Mlle Geneviève Lissert, aged nineteen, who lives in the rue Tourneux in the 12th Arrondissement, yesterday set out for a ride . . .'

I read the rest of the article, then looked through the papers covering the next couple of days. Nothing of interest. I wrote down Mlle Lissert's address.

5 The Girl in the Rue Tourneux

I enquired at the concierge's lodge, then went up the brown-carpeted stairs to the third floor. There was a name-card on the oak door above a spotless brass bell. My ring was answered by a woman who was still young. But her hair was white and her face prematurely aged.

I didn't quite know how to begin. The papers hadn't said whether or not the girl had survived the accident. I had to take a chance.

'I was wondering if I might speak to Mlle Lissert . . . Your daughter I believe? . . . I wanted to ask her some questions about her sad accident last year . . .'

The woman winced.

I handed her my card.

'Nestor Burma, private detective,' she said, handing it back. 'I saw your name in the paper. Come in, monsieur.'

The little hall was comfortable and clean.

'I see you've had an accident too,' observed Mme Lissert.

'It happened at the same place as your daughter's, and to tell you the truth I'm carrying out a kind of personal inquiry of my own. But I'd quite understand if you thought I oughtn't to bother Mlle Lissert . . .'

'Perhaps I could help you instead. Gigi . . . It upsets her to talk about it. What was it you wanted to know, exactly?'

'How the accident happened. The newspapers never give a clear account . . .'

'She couldn't ever make out how it happened,' said the mother, struggling against her tears. 'She was in a car on the scenic railway with some friends, and she thinks she remembers bending forward, and the next thing she knew she was in hospital. With a broken spine, monsieur, and her mind all confused. It was months before she could think or speak properly, and she never *could* say exactly how it happened. And of course we never talk about it . . .'

She was weeping now without restraint. Then she laid a hand on my arm and gazed fiercely into my eyes.

'Do you think it *wasn't* an accident?'

'I don't know, madame.'

'If it was that man . . . the same one that attacked you . . . !'

'If it *was*, he has paid dearly for it, madame. But there's nothing to suggest that what happened to your daughter was anything other than a terrible accident. That's what the police thought, didn't they? . . . I'm so sorry if I've upset you.'

'If it *was* him, and he had accomplices . . . Come, monsieur. Come with me and see what they did to my little girl.'

She led the way into the next room, a sitting room overlooking the avenue Daumesnil. If you leaned out of the window you could see the fountain in the place Félix-Eboué. If you leaned out . . . The other person with us in the room couldn't lean very far now. She was a very pretty girl of about twenty, with long fair hair flowing down over her shoulders. A fine oval face with a delicate nose, and eyes that were bright, though sad. But she had practically no neck, she sat unnaturally upright as though wearing a corset, and her legs, no doubt twisted and atrophied because she could no longer use them, were concealed by a rug. I was looking at all that was left of a lovely young creature born for pleasure and life.

'Gigi,' said the mother, who had regained some of her composure, 'this is Monsieur Nestor Burma . . .' The great limpid eyes lit up. 'An old friend of Father's . . .'

'No, mother,' the girl said softly, 'I heard his name on the radio. I know what happened to him.' She looked at me. 'You were luckier than I was, monsieur.'

I didn't know what to say. As we shook hands I accidentally knocked down a fashion magazine she'd been reading as we came in. I picked it up and handed it back; she smiled wanly at the picture of the girl on the cover. It was May. The time when young women of her age start wearing summer dresses, with low necks and short skirts to show their legs and other charms to advantage. Never again, for her.

Again I was lost for words. It was she who helped me out.

'I expect you'd like me to tell you how it happened?'
'Yes, please . . . Unless . . .'
'Oh, I can't say I've got used to it, or that I'm

resigned to my fate, but I *can* talk about it, especially now I'm beginning to wonder whether *I* wasn't pushed too . . .'

'But you've never said anything before!' sobbed her mother.

'No. It was while I was listening to the radio today . . . I remembered leaning forward to look down at the crowd below . . . and *now* I seem to remember being taken hold of round the waist . . .'

This was all going too fast. I'd come in the hope of hearing evidence of a deliberate attack, but it looked as if the poor girl had merely been influenced in retrospect, by suggestion.

'Just a moment,' I said. 'If anyone tried to push you off the scenic railway they'd need to have a reason. Did you have any enemies?'

'No. But according to the radio, there wasn't any reason for your being pushed, either.'

I smiled.

'I didn't tell the police everything.'

'I see!'

She smiled too. Quick-witted as well as pretty.

'In my case, there really wasn't any reason,' she said. 'I didn't have any enemies.'

'No rejected swain, for example . . . ?'

'No.'

'I believe you were with friends when it happened?'

'Yes.'

'Can you remember who they were?'

'Yes.'

I wrote down three names and addresses. Two boys and a girl.

'Who was sitting behind you?'

'I don't know.'

'One of your friends?'

'No . . . I don't think so.'

'A stranger, then?'

'Perhaps.'

'It happened in the evening, didn't it?'

'Yes. A Monday evening.'

Her lips twitched. Despite her courage, these memories were becoming unbearable.

'As far as I could see from the papers, your accident didn't give rise to much comment at the time.'

'No . . . So I was told, afterwards.'

'The man who fell yesterday was called Lancelin. Do you know anyone of that name?'

'No.'

'It might be a false name. I have a few ideas on the subject. I'm sorry I haven't got a photograph. It might have—'

'Talking of photos!' she said. 'Mother, let's show him our pictures!' Then, turning to me: 'I'd like you to see me as I was before.'

Mme Lissert reluctantly let down a screen, drew the curtains, and started to project a home movie showing Geneviève with a party of friends – including those whose names and addresses I'd just taken down.

'This reel was taken that Sunday afternoon,' she said. 'The day before the accident.'

Then, with a pitiful little laugh: 'This is where Benoît filmed me from behind – he said I walked like Marilyn Monroe. I didn't, did I?'

'Better!' I said inadvertently. 'Not so obviously

provocative, but more dangerous! . . . But I say – your hair wasn't blonde then, was it?'

'No – auburn. Benoît used to tease me and call it ginger, but I'm naturally auburn. I can't think why I changed it.'

Probably just for something to do. The time must go very slowly when you've lost the use of your legs.

The film ended. I opened the curtains. Mme Lissert, still sniffing a little, put the projector away.

'I must be going,' I said. 'Thank you for seeing me.'

'I was pretty, wasn't I?' said Geneviève, her eyes brimming with tears.

'You still are.'

She shrugged wearily and held out her hand. Mme Lissert saw me out.

I went into the first bar I came to and ordered a pastis. A double.

6 *Fernand to the Rescue*

Back at the *Crépu*, Covet was still out on his story. I collected the touched-up picture of the late Roger Lancelin – it was better than I'd expected – together with a couple of the unimproved ones, bought the artist a quick drink, and drove to the 12th Arrondissement. To the rue de la Brèche-aux-Loups.

The girl was as easy on the eye in daylight as she had been in the dusk of the Fair. Easier! Abundant long black hair. Beautiful legs. Simone Blanchet, twenty-five years old, single . . . Occupation? No mention had been made of that. She wasn't at work this afternoon, anyhow.

When I'd identified myself she asked me into a small but tasteful apartment, rather incongruous behind that dilapidated façade. She was obviously curious about me. What could he want with her, this chap who'd been a fellow-passenger yesterday on the same tragic ride as herself, and who according to the radio and the papers – there was a wireless set in one corner, and copies of the *Crépu* and *France-Soir* lay strewn over the divan – was in fact a private eye?

We looked at one another. The more I looked the surer I was she had nothing on under her light-coloured sheath dress.

'How are you getting on?' I asked. 'They told me at the police station last night that you'd fainted at the sight of the struggle, and that when you came to you were still very shaken. As in a way it was all my fault, I thought I'd come round to see how you were and offer my apologies.'

She smiled. 'Thank you. There was no need. I'm perfectly all right now. I *was* frightened, but I've got over it. I just took the opportunity to have a day off from the office. Naughty of me, wasn't it?'

'Oh, I don't know . . . So you work in an office . . .'

'Yes. For the Henri-Marc Wine Company at Bercy.'

'Oh. And is one allowed to meet you there in the evening, on one of the days you do go to work? I'm not going to sue you for damages, but it was partly your fault if I nearly got rubbed out yesterday.'

'My fault? How?'

'You've got such nice legs . . .'

She shifted them a little, but her dress was too scanty to cover them up.

'I noticed them, and followed them, and if *they* hadn't got on to the scenic railway . . .'

I went on chatting her up for a while, then suddenly confronted her with a picture of Lancelin – the presentable version. She didn't bat an eyelid.

'What's this?' she said. 'Your secret weapon?'

'It's Lancelin,' I told her.

'I wouldn't have recognized him if you hadn't told me. Of course, I didn't really get a proper look at him. He wasn't bad-looking, was he? Except for those eyebrows. Too close together. Sly . . .'

'What about these, then?'

I stuck the macabre shots from the morgue in front of her. She gave a little shriek and pushed them away.

'How horrible! What on earth are you showing me *these* for?'

'I'm sorry. I'm not really myself today . . . But may I come and see you again?'

'When you're back to normal? Why not? . . .' She put a hand on mine. 'But I still won't be able to tell you I knew Lancelin, because I didn't. Wasn't that what you wanted to know?'

'Yes.'

'And what would you have deduced if I had known him?'

'I don't know. Be seeing you!'

I went back to my car and sat crouched over the wheel like the idiot I was. I'd imagined the girl in blue knew Lancelin, that the two of them were in league, and that she'd dangled her legs in front of me to lure me on to the switchback. And I'd meant to take her by surprise. But I was the only one who was surprised, and I was no farther forward now than I had been before.

I drove about for a while, then went into a bar and looked up the Henri-Marc Wine Company in the telephone book.

'May I speak to Mlle Simone Blanchet, please?'

'Mlle Blanchet isn't here, monsieur.'

'But she does work there, doesn't she?'

'Yes. Why—'

I hung up, went back to the car, and decided I might as well look up the three friends who had been with Geneviève Lissert when she met with her accident.

I found Philippe Laubert and Josée Roux having an apéritif together in the boulevard de Reuilly. They were no use. It was all such a long time ago, wasn't it? Besides, we told the police everything we knew at the time. We didn't notice Gigi had disappeared until we got off . . . Hey, we're not going to be bothered all over again because of what happened yesterday, are we? It would have been better if we'd let Gigi go to the Fair on her own . . .

I produced Lancelin's photograph. Doubtful expressions . . . It *was* a year ago, you know . . .

Jacques Benoît lived in the rue Albert-Malet, on the far side of the Square Georges-Méliès. A strapping young man of twenty-four, neither handsome nor ugly, but attractive. Frank and direct – blunt, even. His voice was very intense when he talked about Geneviève. He still saw her. They'd slept together before the accident. She was the one who didn't want them to get married now, but he hadn't changed his mind, and whenever she wanted . . .

Congratulations, young man. But what about 7 May 1956? His account of what happened that evening was no more use than that of his friends had been.

'Whereabouts were you sitting?'

'I don't remember.'

'You weren't in the seat just behind Gigi? Seeing she was your girlfriend . . .'

'We'd had a row . . . What fools people are sometimes, eh?'

'Yes. Often. Too often . . . So who was sitting behind Gigi, then?'

'A stranger. Wait a minute . . . I seem to remember he jostled the rest of us aside in order to sit there.'

'People are always jostling one another to get a seat. Especially when they're young and boisterous.'

'Perhaps.'

I showed him the picture of Lancelin. He didn't recognize it. I hadn't expected him to. It had all happened a year ago, and no one had ever paid much attention to the man who'd sat behind Gigi.

I went back to my car, depressed. Why? What did I expect? That someone would say yes, that's Lancelin: he was the one sitting behind Gigi, and it was he who threw her off the scenic railway, and he knew this person and that . . . Then I would go and see this person and that, and with a bit of luck they'd tell me why Lancelin had come up to Paris from Marseilles, and also why he'd tried to get rid of me. And whatever that taught me, I'd serve it up on a platter to Faroux and Grégoire and enjoy the look on their faces.

Some hopes!

As I puffed thoughtfully at my pipe, I remembered Faroux's suggestion about getting myself a girl. It was an idea. I took off in the direction of the rue de la Brèche-aux-Loups.

Simone Blanchet was in, though apparently dressed to go out. If that was the right expression: she didn't seem to be wearing very much. She greeted me with evident pleasure, as if she'd been expecting me. I'd clicked and no mistake.

'You said I could come back when I was better,' I

said, 'and I am. So if you're free . . . But perhaps you were going somewhere?'

'No – I've just come in. I had an errand to do. You might easily have missed me.'

'If you hadn't taken a taxi, for instance,' I said, trying to impress her.

She looked duly astonished.

'How in the world . . . ?'

Then, crossly: 'You've been following me! That's not nice!'

'No, I haven't.'

'Well, then, you saw me getting out of the cab.'

'Nope. I just saw that. That was enough.'

I pointed to her handbag, thrown down on the divan. It had come open as it fell, and among some hundred-franc notes that were spilling out I could see a business card belonging to the Taxito Taxi Company.

I passed it to her.

'The driver must have given it to me with my change,' she said. 'But I might easily have had it in my bag for a fortnight!'

'Absolutely. One must never jump to conclusions. But I would like to come to a conclusion with you! As I was saying, if you're free we might have dinner together.'

'So that I conclude by getting drunk, and you wring a confession from me?'

'Something, anyway.'

As we talked she undulated about the room in a vampish manner, toying with various objects, till I almost felt I was back on the scenic railway. And after some more stalling she accepted my invitation.

'I've never been out with a private detective before. It must be very interesting.'

'As you noticed yesterday.'

'And what are we going to do after dinner?'

'I thought we might drop in at the Fair.'

'Why, do you feel like killing someone else?'

A few more minutes of this brilliant repartee and we were ready to set off. It was a fine evening, and as Simone wasn't afraid of the cold she made a nice eyeful. We had a leisurely dinner in a good restaurant, chatting like old acquaintances, and after she'd retired for a moment to powder her nose, which looked perfect as it was, we drove to the place de la Nation.

The Fair was as loud and colourful as before. We patronized some of the more peaceful sideshows, avoiding the scenic railway. We went and felt the calves of the Young Giantess. We watched the tableaux vivants, where girls posing in G-strings the size of Bermudas gossiped between themselves and scratched uninhibitedly, regardless of the audience. We also went and saw the two 'native' fire-eaters, who after straightening 'red-hot' iron bars, and so on, proceeded to eat a flaming 'lion sausage'.

Simone and I were standing among a group of unsavoury-looking, loud-shirted young rowdies, the sort who should never be allowed to drink, and they now began to bawl out that the show was a fake. Everyone else went on watching intently. If it *was* only an illusion, it was an illusion skilfully produced.

Suddenly Simone swung round and gave the youth standing behind her a resounding box on the ear. He just sniggered.

'Hey – she isn't wearing any pants!'

General hilarity.

'Shut up!' hissed one spectator, anxious not to miss any of the show.

'She hasn't got any pants on!' the lout repeated, nudging one of his pals. The lout was an albino, with thin, mean lips and the rheumy eyes of a wino. But I don't think he was really tipsy: his father, grandfather and great-grandfather had done his drinking for him, and he was the one who puked. His friend was a head taller – a burly, fairly handsome youth with eyes that were meant to look cruel but were really only stupid.

Behind these two beauties milled an assortment of similar specimens.

'Take it easy, my lad,' I said. 'And keep your hands to yourself.'

'Yes, monsieur,' mocked the albino.

Before all this could go any further the showman announced that the fire-eating display was over, and the yokels barged out in front of everyone else.

'Let's get out of here,' said Simone after we'd left the tent. 'I like fairs usually, but it's unbearable with all these yobs about.'

We pushed through the people now making their way into the next fire-eating session, only to find ourselves confronted by the albino and his friend, plus a third and equally revolting ruffian. When they resumed their taunts about Simone, I started after them, but she restrained me.

'Please! Leave it! Just let's go!'

So we walked on down the cours de Vincennes,

threading our way through the crowds, the shooting galleries and the hoop-la stalls, then on through the trees and behind the caravans.

'Hi! Is it true that you're not wearing any pants, darling? Will you let us see?'

The louts must have followed us. I turned round. There were about half a dozen of them. I fell on the nearest one, who happened to be the albino, and got him by the scruff of his red shirt.

His burly pal put a paw on my chest to shove me away.

'All right, pop – we're not looking for trouble.'

I knocked his hand away roughly.

'Can't you take a joke?' he growled. 'I said we weren't looking for trouble!'

But by now I was. I lashed out, he lashed back, and in a moment the rest of the gang mixed in and we were all rolling on the ground, six against one. And no holds barred as far as they were concerned. Fists and knees and leather belts were coming at me from all sides, and usually hitting their mark. I'd just got hold of one chap by what must have been his nose when a hefty blow landed where it matters most, and I doubled up. If this went on much longer . . .

'Hey, Bébert!' someone shouted. 'Is that how you try to show you're a man? Go on, clear off, the lot of you!'

As through a mist I saw a huge half-naked chap wade into the youths and send them packing single-handed. Then he came over to me.

'They're beginning to get on my wick,' he said, picking me up as if I were a feather and propping me against a tree. 'I got here just in time, eh? Six against one, the swine!'

My saviour was a huge bruiser with close-cropped fair hair, a broken nose and cauliflower ears. A five-pointed star was tattooed on the back of the carpet-beater he used as a hand, and he had a broad leather band round his wrist. That was all he *was* wearing, apart from trainers and a pair of black silk shorts trimmed with white.

'I was having a snooze in the caravan,' he said, 'when those bastards woke me up . . .' He yawned or grimaced, perhaps both, and rubbed his belly. 'You'd better wash the mud off your kisser.'

'There was someone with me. A girl. Have you seen her?'

'She's over there, on a bench.'

'Passed out?'

'Don't think so.'

A soft and trembling hand was placed on my aching arm.

'I'm sorry,' stammered Simone. 'It was all my fault . . .'

'Forget it,' I said.

The providential wrestler, whose name turned out to be Fernand, spoke again.

'Better come to my place', he said, 'to wash the mud off your kisser and see no bones are broken.'

Next thing I knew – had he tucked me under his arm like a parcel? – I was lying on a narrow bed in Fernand's caravan.

'I was just having a snooze,' he repeated. 'I'm not working tonight because I ate something that didn't agree with me.' He massaged his paunch again. 'Luckily for you. The cops would have turned up in the end. But when?'

I looked at Simone, who was sitting by the bed. 'You didn't think of that,' I said.

'What?'

'Fetching the police.'

'Don't mention them!' said Fernand. 'We're better off without them.'

'We did manage,' I agreed.

'I . . . I was rooted to the spot,' said Simone. 'It all happened so quickly!'

'It seemed like a long time to me!'

Meanwhile the wrestler was prodding me from top to toe with his vast mitts.

'OK,' he said at last. 'Nothing broken. Just a little going-over. But we'd better clean up your clock.'

He went and fetched a bowl of water and a sponge.

'I'll do it,' said Simone. And she set to gently and bathed my face as if she'd been doing it all her life. The wrestler sat on a stool and smoked a Gauloise. He didn't regret having come to my rescue. We both had an excellent view down the front of Simone's dress.

'Who were those louts?' I asked.

'Oh, you always get a couple of gangs like that at every fair,' he said scornfully. 'Bold enough when they're only harassing women, but no real guts . . . How are you feeling now?'

'Better.'

'S'nothing serious. Just a little going-over. How about a drink?'

'Yes, please. Anything will do, with a couple of aspirin.'

We drank and chatted, and before long I felt well enough to be on my way.

'Well, goodbye, Fernand. And thanks for happening along.'

'Any time!' he said, as our hands disappeared in his carpet-beaters.

With some assistance from Simone I tottered back to the car, breathing a sigh of relief as I settled behind the wheel. Despite her protestations about my state of health, I drove her home. Then, as we drew up outside her house: 'Simone,' I said, 'I'm feeling really rotten. I don't think I've got the strength to drive to my place. Would you let me stay the night here, if you don't think it would compromise you? You needn't worry – one of those knights-errant has neutralized the danger zone for the time being . . .'

'Don't be silly! Of course you can stay. After all, it *was* my fault . . .'

And she helped me up the stairs. 'You take the divan,' she said. 'There's a convertible armchair in the other room – I'll sleep there.'

I flopped down fully dressed. 'Some enchanted evening, eh?' I laughed. 'Well, you said yourself it must be interesting to go out with a private detective! Ye gods, my head! Have you got any aspirin?'

She brought me three with a glass of water.

'Get thee behind me, *femme fatale*!' I said.

'What do you mean?'

I said I thought I must be feverish.

It was funny, though. She looked just like my sort

of girl, but had she got the evil eye or something? Whenever I came near her something happened. Yesterday the scenic railway. Today the fight.

She went out into the hall. I could hear her bolting the front door.

'Goodnight. Sleep well!' she said on her way to the other room.

'I certainly shall with you near by!' I answered, gallant as ever. Then I heard her lock that door too. A vote of confidence. Well, it was mutual. I switched the light off and let an hour go by, counting my bruises, then switched the light on again, got up stealthily, and searched the room. I felt rather ashamed of myself, but I did it just the same. I didn't know what I was looking for exactly, and anyhow I didn't find anything.

Then I lay down again, and this time slept – undeservedly – the sleep of the just.

7 Leads on Lancelin

A hand shook me by the shoulder. I opened my eyes. Daylight. Simone was standing by the divan, dressed ready to go out. She couldn't stay away from work indefinitely, could she? Of course not. A cup of coffee? Yes, please.

I drank it and got up, then went to splash my face with cold water in the bathroom, amid the scents of Simone's beauty aids. I looked in the mirror: the face of the famous crack detective looked like a slice of mouldy mortadella. I prodded myself. A lot of sensitive spots still. Just a little going-over, eh? I joined Simone for another cup of coffee.

'How do you feel?'

'All right. May I drive you to work? I know I'm not a very elegant escort—' I pointed to my suit. It too had suffered in the fray, not to mention the fact that I'd slept in it '—but it'll be all right if I don't get out of the car!'

'All right. Thanks.'

She smiled. 'And it'll give you a chance to check that I really do work where I said I did, won't it?'

'I don't need to check,' said I. 'I phoned your office yesterday.'

It was nine-thirty when I got to my own office. The Fiat Lux Agency. Inquiries of All Kinds. Director: Yours Truly.

As I was still going up the stairs between the first and second floors, something made me look up.

Leaning over the banister above me were two sets of hats and coats which would have liked to pass unnoticed. The inevitable Inspector Grégoire and a colleague.

'Hallo!' I called. 'Have you come to consult me professionally?'

'Too right!' Grégoire answered. 'But what happened to your face?'

'I always look like that the morning after.'

'The morning after what? The Foire du Trône?'

'That's right. I made a pass at the Bearded Lady and this is what I got for it.'

'Ha ha. The truth, if you don't mind.'

'I walked into a door.'

Before I could open my own door, Grégoire and his pal had come down on to my landing. I invited them in, but they declined.

'We've wasted enough time already,' said Grégoire. 'So you can stop beating about the bush and come along with us to the Quai des Orfèvres.'

I was too exhausted to argue. I didn't even ask them to let me change my clothes (I keep some of my things at the office). Anyhow, perhaps it's better not to look too spruce when you're hauled up before the CID.

★

53

Florimond Faroux let out an oath when he saw me.

'Good God! Where did you get that face?'

After a few pleasantries I gave him the true explanation.

'I was set on by a gang of youths at the Foire du Trône. Yobs that you ought to get your colleagues in the 12th arrondissement on to. Louts who think it's amusing to pinch women's bottoms.'

Faroux sighed. 'If *we* had to pinch all the bottom-pinchers, there wouldn't be anyone out of gaol . . . Now, let's be serious.'

He glanced at the portrait of the Prefect of Police that hung on the wall of his office, presumably to supply his subordinates with inspiration. Then he looked back at my two shiners.

'You don't seem able to keep away from the Foire du Trône, do you? Do you find it all that amusing?'

'I don't plan all my movements.'

'H'm . . . Are you working for someone, or just poking your nose into something that's none of your business?'

'I'm not working for anyone.'

'I suppose not – if you were, they'd have let us know. Right, then – you don't need to cover for anyone, but still you won't come clean with us. So you must be just trying to get in our hair by working for yourself and meddling in what doesn't concern you . . . Bring in the other weirdo, Grégoire.'

The newcomer was a brawny fellow in handcuffs. He was wearing scruffy jeans, a loud jacket, and a forbidding scowl. Frizzy hair, narrow forehead, shifty eyes, big nose, jug ears and no lips. His complexion suggested he'd come straight out of a police cell.

'You said you wanted to see Nestor Burma,' Faroux told him. 'Well, here he is. And if you want to talk to him, now's your chance.'

The other shook his head. 'I got nothing to say,' he croaked, 'and I don't understand a word of all your poppycock.'

'You can take him back to the others, then, Grégoire,' said the Superintendent, 'and let them get on with the questioning.'

'What was all that about?' I asked when Grégoire and his charge had gone away again.

By way of reply Faroux took some photographs out of a file and handed them to me. They showed a rather nasty, not over-bright piece of work, flashily dressed, who seemed vaguely familiar.

'That's Pascal Troyenny, a Marseilles hood,' said Faroux. 'As he was a year or two ago. Changed a bit, hasn't he?'

'You don't mean . . .'

'Yes – the chap you saw just now.'

Grégoire came in again.

'Is he singing or not?' asked his boss.

'No. Not yet . . . But even if he knows some tricks for walking unscathed on red-hot coals, I bet he doesn't know any for holding out against the team that's working on him now!'

'What!' I exclaimed. 'Do you mean to say Troyenny is—'

'A fire-eater, yes. At the Foire du Trône,' said Faroux. 'That's why we arrested him.'

I scratched my head. 'I don't see the connection.'

'I'll explain. Yesterday afternoon we were collecting information about the mysterious Lancelin. It turns out he was already on our files – a few thefts and suchlike before the war, he called himself Roger Lecanut in those days – his true name, as it happens, and he doesn't really come from Marseilles . . . But perhaps you know all this already?'

I assured him I didn't. I wasn't sure he believed me.

'Anyhow, he seems to have settled down after the war started – at least, he didn't add anything to his record with us. But we wired his fingerprints to Marseilles, and at the end of the afternoon we had a reply.'

'Interesting?'

'Very. So much so that I sent Grégoire and another officer round to ask you for some further information. I was thinking about the reward.'

'Is there a reward?'

'There is,' said Faroux severely, 'and I want to warn you once and for all to be content with that when you're not working for someone else! Instead of trying to solve the case all by yourself and then getting your pal Covet to write an article saying how clever you are, and how long it takes the police to get nowhere! When you have any information concerning a case in which you're not professionally involved, it's your duty to pass that information on to us. Understand?'

'OK, OK . . .'

'Well, I sent Grégoire and Langlois round to see you. You weren't in, either at your flat or at your office, so they waited for you. You tell him what happened, Grégoire.'

'We decided to wait at your office,' said the inspector, 'and in the middle of the night someone turned up. He looked pretty shady. I smelled a rat.'

'As usual,' said I.

'I asked if he lived there. He didn't seem very sure. I asked for his papers. He looked furtive. When I asked him about his job he said he worked as a 'native' fire-eater at the Foire du Trône. Then I started to prick up my ears.

' "Are you here to see the detective, by any chance?" I asked him.

' "Nestor Burma?" says he. "Never heard of him!"

'Pretty dumb, eh?

'We took him in charge, and after we got him here we found he was Pascal Troyenny, suspected of a couple of killings in Montpellier eight months ago. He was carrying a gun and a bag of tools for breaking and entering.'

'So he came to my place intending to burgle my office?'

'Maybe.'

Faroux now took over again. 'And we'd like to know what the connection is between you and these two criminals, Lancelin and Troyenny.'

'Were they friends?'

'Accomplices. I don't think you ever met Troyenny. But I'm not so sure about you and Lancelin . . .'

'We met on the scenic railway,' I said bitterly. 'As at least a thousand people can testify.'

'You met there for the first time?'

'And the last.'

Faroux thumped his desk.

'Then for crying out loud why did he try to do you in? And on the scenic railway, of all places?'

I sighed. 'I'm getting a bit fed up with all your suspicions. But I'm not going to defy you, because if I did I wouldn't be able to buy a packet of tobacco without having you behind me to find out what I was really up to. Nor am I going to tell you why Lancelin chose the scenic railway to try to get rid of me. But I *will* tell you why he *did* want to get rid of me.'

'Marvellous! You *do* know why, do you?'

'I've only got a theory on the subject, but I think it's correct, even though there are still gaps in it that need to be filled in. Here it is, for what it's worth. Lancelin is summoned to Paris for something important. I don't know what it is, but it must be important.'

'Very important.'

'Oh? You know what it is?'

'We have an idea. Go on.'

'Lancelin arrives at the Gare de Lyon and catches sight of Grégoire and me, apparently a typical couple of cops. Later the same evening, at the Foire du Trône, where he may have gone for some reason or other to see his pal the fire-eater, he spots me again and thinks I must be following him. And so, as this is the last thing he wants, he tries to kill me.'

'But why on the scenic railway?'

'Ask me another!'

Faroux frowned and stroked his moustache.

'But why? What was the point of killing just you? According to your hypothesis he saw two of you at the Gare de Lyon. And he must have deduced that you weren't the only ones.'

'Yes. But I was alone at the Fair. Maybe he thought I was the one who knew everything. You don't have a monopoly on suspicion.'

Faroux pondered. A long silence. The portrait of the

Prefect of Police seemed to be giving us his blessing.

'We've been in touch with Cannes,' Faroux said. 'And I must admit they tell us your Hélène has been there for the last three weeks. And that she was supposed to have caught the train in question, but couldn't because she'd sprained her ankle.'

'Thanks,' I said. 'I was afraid she'd picked up a banker.'

Another silence. Then Faroux pointed a tobacco-stained finger at my damaged face. 'And what about that? Has that got anything to do with anything, or was it just an accident?'

'It was an accident. I was at the fair with a girlfriend. Some young yob bothered her, I protested, and they fell on me, six to one. As I told you before. You can easily check.'

'Right,' said Faroux. 'I reckon you're being reasonably straightforward as far as Lancelin is concerned. It's a bit vague, but no doubt it'll all come out in the end. I don't think you're trying to have us on.'

I said nothing. If I agreed it might reopen the whole question.

'But we must have whetted your appetite now, and I suppose if I don't tell you everything you'll be prowling around trying to ferret it out for yourself. And that's strictly not on . . . So listen . . . Did you hear about some gold being stolen, a hundred and fifty kilos of it, at the Gare de Rondelet at Montpellier about eight months ago?'

'Vaguely.'

'Well, we have reason to suppose Troyenny and Lecanut, otherwise known as Lancelin, were mixed up in it, together with some others. But until now we couldn't track them down. Or the swag, either.'

'Can't you go into a bit more detail?' I asked.

'I don't see why I should bother. You can look the case up in the papers . . . Speaking of which, we don't want it known that we've nabbed Troyenny, nor that we've got a new angle on Lancelin. And if any reporter, including Marc Covet, lets either cat out of the bag, I shall hold you responsible. So you just keep your nose clean, my friend. You're welcome to go after the reward, but any new information you come across must be passed on to me straight away.'

'OK. What's come over you? Change of life or something?'

'Never you mind.'

'I assume, then, that the lost gold may be somewhere around, and that Lancelin came to Paris to collect his share?'

'Probably.'

'And what do you think Troyenny was doing at my place?'

'I don't know yet. And since you don't either, we can't ask you. But we can ask *him*!'

'And he'll tell us, by God!' said Grégoire fiercely. 'That and the rest!'

'The rest? What do you mean by that?'

'Everything!' said Faroux. 'He'll admit he took part in the robbery – so far he stoutly denies it. And also . . . well, everything!'

'Including where they stashed the gold?'

'Why not?'

I laughed. 'No way!'

'Why do you say that?'

'My dear Florimond, everyone involved in this case keeps thinking I know more than I do. You, Grégoire, Lancelin – and Troyenny. He *might* have come to my place to avenge his friend – after all, I *was* the immediate cause of Lancelin's falling to his death. But I don't think it was that. I think he must have read the papers and come to the conclusion that I was in league with Lancelin and knew where the gold was – in fact, that that was why I killed him. And so along he came to remind me of his own claim . . .'

'If so he can't have a very high opinion of the probity of private detectives!'

'He's not the only one!' I said, looking meaningly at Grégoire. 'Anyhow, if I'm right, you can question Troyenny till you're blue in the face, with a pneumatic drill if you like, he won't tell you where the gold is. Because he doesn't know.'

'We'll see,' said Faroux. 'Meanwhile, *you* can go. But remember what I said.'

8 The Key

I went back to my office to change. The Foire du Trône was costing me a pretty penny: a hat lost the other night, a suit ruined yesterday . . . After lunch I spent a few hours at the Bibliothèque Nationale, looking up press accounts of the gold robbery.

September 1956
A siding at the Montpellier-Rondelet railway station. An ordinary-looking truck. But it contains millions of francsworth of gold ingots belonging to the Paris Precious Metals Consortium, and is watched over by a couple of armed guards. But next morning at dawn a railwayman discovers their lifeless bodies. They've been shot, apparently by guns fitted with silencers; the truck has been broken into; some of the ingots are missing. Despite investigations both in Montpellier and in Paris, the police can't identify the murderers or find out where the gold has gone to.

A few days go by.

Some children playing on the beach at Palavas, a few miles from Montpellier, find two gold ingots buried in the sand. But digging up the beach produces no more. The police assume that the swag was put on a boat that is now cruising somewhere around the Mediterranean. But they can't find it.

More days go by.

By chance, a man called Troyenny is arrested in Marseilles, carrying a revolver. He manages to escape, leaving behind not only his gun but also evidence that he was in Montpellier for a few days at the time of the robbery. Ballistic checks show that the bullets in the gun correspond to those that killed the two guards. But the cops are unable to find either Troyenny or the stolen gold. The Paris Precious Metals Consortium offers a handsome reward, but without result.

More days go by.

Weeks.

Months.

No mention in all this of Lecanut, subsequently known as Lancelin. Perhaps the cops in the south had had some reason for not mentioning him. Perhaps they didn't find out until later that he might be involved, and I myself had missed any current reference. But what did it matter? Faroux had told me both Lancelin and Troyenny were connected with the robbery, and that no doubt there were others involved. Others who must be in Paris to share out the swag now that the time was ripe. And who, if I could trace them, would lead me to the reward.

That would compensate me for the scare I'd had, for having to buy a new hat and send my suit to the

cleaner's, and for the annoyances inflicted on me by
Faroux and his boys.

I left the studious silence of the Bibliothèque Nationale
for the din of a nearby café, where I thought things
over to the accompaniment of several juke-boxes.

It all came back to the scenic railway. It wasn't the
obvious place for knocking someone off, but Lecanut-
Lancelin had chosen it for getting shot of me. Well,
not exactly chosen it – he didn't force me to take a ride
on it. He just took advantage of the opportunity I gave
him to exercise his talents. Yes, his talents. If he seized
the chance I offered him, it must have been because it
wasn't his first attempt at this sort of thing. For I
couldn't get rid of the idea that instead of being the
victim of a mere accident, Geneviève had been deliberately thrown off the scenic railway. She said she hadn't
any enemies. But a person can have enemies without
suspecting it. Enemies who hide their true feelings.
Until . . .

It seemed to me I ought to go back to the rue Tourneux for a little checking up. But for that I needed the
photograph of Lecanut, and I'd left it in the pocket of
the suit I was wearing the day before. So back I went
to the office.

Just as I was about to leave, the phone rang.

'Monsieur Nestor Burma?'

'Speaking.'

'At last! . . . Charles Montolieu here . . . I'd like
you to do a small job for me . . . If you're not too
busy . . . I've been trying to reach you ever since yesterday and you were never in . . .'

'But I'm not too busy! What was it you wanted me to do, exactly?'

'It would take too long to explain over the phone. In any case it would be better for us to meet, don't you think?'

'Certainly, if you wish.'

'This evening at eight? That do?'

'Right. Your place or mine?'

'Mine.'

He gave an address in the avenue de Saint-Mandé.

My jaw dropped. 'That's in the 12th Arrond-issement!'

My reaction must have been audible. 'Yes,' said the man at the other end of the line, 'but don't worry. It won't be as dangerous as the scenic railway.'

'What makes you say that?' I snapped.

'. . . I do read the papers, monsieur,' he said. As if to imply that otherwise he wouldn't have known I existed. There's glory for you.

'Very well,' I said. 'Until this evening.'

'Lecanut,' I said. 'Roger Lecanut. Does the name remind you of anything?'

I looked from Mme Lissert's face to that of her daughter. Neither hesitated. No, the name meant nothing to them.

I showed them the photograph.

'No – I've never met him,' said Mme Lissert.

'Neither have I,' said Geneviève. 'Do you . . . do you think this might have been the man who sat behind me on the switchback last year?'

'Yes . . . Maybe . . .'

She sighed. 'There *was* someone. But it wasn't anyone I knew. And I couldn't say what he looked like, or whether that's a photograph of him or not.'

I put the photograph away and stood up to leave.

'What happened to you?' the girl asked.

'What ha— Oh, you mean my face?'

Mme Lissert looked at her daughter reproachfully. She must have noticed my bruises too, but it wasn't really done to make personal remarks.

'I had another fight at the Fair,' I said. 'With some louts who insulted a girl I was with. Was there—' it probably wouldn't get me anywhere, but it was just worth a try – 'Was there a bunch of louts like that at the Fair last year?'

She looked at me in surprise. 'There always is, isn't there?'

It was around seven-thirty when I arrived at the Foire du Trône. By way of a change. There weren't many people there yet, and not all of the stands were open. The fire-eaters Simone and I had visited the day before had already started their show. It wasn't the one where Troyenny worked. That was in a similar set-up opposite, which was now closed: its owners had probably been summoned to see Faroux at the Quai des Orfèvres.

Things were quite quiet on the scenic railway too. Though that wasn't why I'd come, perhaps now was a good moment to try to recover my hat: for I'd noticed a chap in a blue tracksuit leaning over the rail by the landing stage, waiting for things to warm up. I went closer. It was the fellow who'd given me a stool to sit on when I felt faint, and who'd been brought along as a witness to the police station in the rue du Rendez-Vous.

'Hallo!' he called when he saw me. 'Come back for your hat?'

'Is it still wearable?'

'Just about. Come and have a look.'

As he led the way to his caravan he glanced at my face and said: 'Did he hit you as hard as that, then?'

'No,' I told him. 'I did this afterwards. Talk about a chapter of accidents!'

He didn't enquire any further. Inside his caravan he produced a rather battered object.

'Not too bad, is it?' he said. 'Just brush the mud off and have it pressed.'

I slipped him a tip.

'Oh, and is this yours too?'

He got a bunch of keys out of a drawer.

'I found them on the ground some distance from the body. I thought they must belong either to him or to you. Was it them he hit you with to try to make you let go of him?'

'Could be.'

I looked at the keys more closely. The bunch consisted of two small ordinary keys and one large and ancient-looking one with an intricate head . . . Anything that had belonged to Lecanut might be useful.

'What do you reckon it fits?' I asked.

'Some big gate or other, I'd say.'

'Do the cops know about your find?'

'What good would it be to them?'

'Not much, I suppose. Nor to me. But for me it has got a sort of sentimental value . . .'

To cut a long story short, I bought the bunch of keys from him and made him a present of the hat. As I made my way back up the avenue du Trône I noticed the other caravan, the one where I'd been given first aid, and there sure enough, sitting on a stool outside it in a scruffy bathrobe, with a bucket between his legs, a potato in one hand and a knife in the other, was my saviour. He recognized me. I'd been all too easy to recognize since my battering the previous night.

'Hi!' he said. 'Feeling any better?'

'OK, thanks. What about your innards?'

'Not too bad. They're grateful you asked.'

Cheerful as ever, he put a huge tattooed paw on the place in my jacket where I carry my gun.

'Still got it on you, eh?'

'Noticed it yesterday, did you?'

'Could hardly help it when I was feeling for broken bones, could I? Hell, if you'd produced it last night those yobs would have disappeared double quick!'

'I didn't get the chance – they all piled in so fast! Just as well, though. I was so furious I might have used it. And that's not what I carry it for.'

'Oh.'

'No. You didn't say anything,' I remarked.

'None of my business.'

He sat down and picked up another spud. 'I don't butt into other people's affairs,' he said.

'What a pity,' I replied, 'because I was going to ask you to do just that.'

'Ask away and we'll see.'

I found a crate lying about near by and sat down facing him. There was another knife handy too, so I picked it up, got a potato out of the bucket, and started peeling.

'I'll start by telling you who I am. It's only fair. I'm a private eye. Nothing to do with the regular police.'

'I should hope not.'

He frowned.

'A private eye . . . It wasn't you . . . ?'

'Yes. I was the one involved in that business on the scenic railway the day before yesterday.'

'You don't say!'

He chortled. 'Huh, and then a battle royal the day after! What have you got in mind for today?'

'I thought of taking the louts on again, but one by one this time.'

'Watch out for the eyes!'

'Is that what they aim for?'

'No – I meant the spuds . . . Be a bit more careful, please! As for the yobs, I reckon it'll be some time before they show their ugly faces round here again . . . Especially if . . . Did your scrap with them have anything to do with what happened on the scenic railway?'

He might not meddle with what didn't concern him, but like everyone else he liked to know!

'That's exactly what I've been wondering! Are they the sort of chaps who'd beat someone up if they were paid to?'

I tossed my spud into the bucket and took another.

'You never know,' said the wrestler.

'I'd like to get hold of one of them and ask.'

A pause.

'I was under the impression it was all because of your girlfriend. I thought the row boiled up because they'd pinched her bottom.'

'If the chap who's with the girl in question objects, that gives you a good excuse for beating him up, doesn't it? Anyhow, I'd like to come across them again. They owe me a return match.'

'I understand.'

'When you came on the scene you said something. Something like: "So, Bébert – is that how you try to prove you're a man?" Bébert – was that just any old name, or were you talking to someone in particular?'

He let me finish peeling my current potato before he answered.

'He was someone I knew. And if you knock his block off it'll serve him right. Last year he worked here as stooge in our show – you know, pretending to be a member of the public and challenging the wrestlers to a bout. But sometimes he'd want to impress a pal of his or some bird, and then he'd forget the arrangement and try to take our bloke by surprise. Not that it made much difference to *me* personally – an arranged scrap is more restful, but I can hold my own all right in a real fight.'

He flexed his muscles under his bathrobe.

'Yes, I've seen you . . . And where is this beauty to be found?'

He scratched his head with the handle of his knife. 'Last year he lived in a street leading off the rue de Reuilly. The cour Saint-Charles, the passage Saint-Charles . . . something like that. Opposite a church. He might still be there.'

'I'll go and have a look. But there must be dozens of Béberts around there. Do you know his surname?'

'Millot – at least, that's what he said.'

'Well, I'll be off then. Thanks for the info.' I handed him back the potato I'd been peeling. 'Here – you finish it!'

'I'll have to. Look at this ruddy great speck you've left in!'

'The watchful eye of the law,' I said.

You went through a low archway and the depressing spectacle of the cour Saint-Charles lay before you. Poky little houses on either side, wooden sheds serving as workshops, gutters running with dirty water, uneven cobblestones, lines of ragged washing strung across the windows. And a smell to match the rest. I asked a lad if he knew Albert Millot, and he said no, but there was a Mme Millot who lived on the first floor of a house further along.

The rickety door was answered by a poorly dressed woman who must have been about fifty but looked older.

'What do you want?' she growled. If she'd had better teeth she'd have bitten me.

'Good day. Mme Millot?'

'Yes.'

'I'd like to speak to Albert.'

'You can tell him to go to hell!'

'Gladly, but I have to see him first. Do you know where he is?'

'To hell with you too! I don't even want to hear his name. He cleared out of here months ago . . . What do you want him for?'

'To knock his block off.'

'In that case I wish I *could* tell you where to find him! If you do track him down you can beat him up twice – once for you and once for me!'

She put a trembling hand on my arm. Her eyes filled with tears, whether from grief or from drink I couldn't tell.

'God forgive me – what a way for a mother to talk!'

I extricated myself as best I could, and in so doing nearly fell over someone who seemed to be having a nap on the stairs. I cursed.

I ought to go and start all over again in America, I thought. If I was to believe what I read, private eyes over there spent their time slurping up expensive whisky and mixing with millionaires and glamorous dames. And what did I get? Old mother Millot and the cour Saint-Charles.

The person I'd tripped over seemed to be calling me. He turned out to be a stunted little creature of about fifteen.

'I heard what you were saying just now,' he said. 'And if you want to bash Bébert's face in, I can help you. I owe him one, too!'

'Did he beat you up?'

'Yes. And I know where he and his pals have been meeting since he left home. I can take you there if you like. But it's quite a long way.'

'I've got a car.'

My pocket guide's name was Etienne, and from the directions he gave me it was obvious he wasn't used to travelling by car. As we went along he told me about Bébert and his gang, and how they met in an old railway truck on some waste ground near Saint-Mandé. They didn't live there, of course . . . I wondered if I wasn't just as likely to come across Bébert at the Foire du Trône. Still, as we were on our way . . . On familiar ground again, too. The rue Albert-Malet, where Geneviève Lissert's boyfriend lived, wasn't far off. Could there be any connection between Jacques Benôit and Bébert Millot?

We were now in the avenue Emile-Laurent. On one side were blocks of fairly expensive flats with neat gardens and lawns, and on the other a railway line and a sort of no man's land.

'Here,' said Etienne.

On the right a wood yard. On the left a building site. In between, though probably not for long, a patch of waste ground overgrown with weeds. And in the middle of that, between a couple of dusty bushes, something that had once been a goods truck.

The sliding door was open. That didn't necessarily mean there was anyone inside – perhaps it wouldn't shut.

9 *Taking Off*

In the distance some children were playing, chasing one another round a shack that seemed to have been converted into a makeshift home.

I looked back at the truck. Ah, so somebody lived there too. A young woman had just emerged from it. She walked to and fro for a bit, as if to stretch her legs, then went over to the shack. She moved very gracefully even over that rough ground. A pleasure to watch. Then she came back to the truck, carrying a saucepan.

Suddenly the air was rent by a booming sound behind me. The girl waved her saucepan, which glittered in the sun. A motor scooter roared down the avenue Emile-Laurent, swept past my car, then clattered over the waste ground and came to a halt in front of the truck. As soon as the rider dismounted, the girl jumped on to the scooter in his place and started careering joyfully round the empty space, her hair flying in the wind.

I turned to Etienne.

'That's Bébert,' he said. 'I recognized him as he went by. I didn't know he had a scooter.'

'Just bought it in the flea market, I expect. What about the girl?'

'Can't see her face from here.'

'Is he married?'

'He tries to pick up a girl every year at the Fair. Sometimes he succeeds, sometimes he doesn't.'

'And what about that shack – what's that?'

'Don't know.'

I opened the door of the car. 'Coming?' I asked.

He pulled a face.

'All right. You wait here.'

I tried to edge round by the shack and come up to the truck from behind. Meanwhile the girl had ended her joyride, put the scooter away under a small awning, and followed the youth inside the truck. I crept round the outside and went in myself.

'Greetings, ladies and gentlemen!' I said politely.

A hole in one wall let in a certain amount of light. A certain amount of rain and wind too, no doubt. The place had been made reasonably habitable by means of a new-looking camp bed and some inflatable mattresses. The rest of the furniture, apart from a little campstool, consisted of packing cases. A stove was supported on one of them, and as I entered, Bébert rose from another.

Instead of the red shirt he sported on ceremonial occasions, he now wore blue dungarees. They matched the azure hue of his nose since it had come in contact with my knee.

While still keeping an eye on him, I also inspected the girl.

She'd been lying on the bed, but had sat up abruptly

as I came in, her skirt riding up to reveal shapely bare legs. She was about twenty, with an excellent figure, reddish hair and a pretty little face with high cheekbones and no make-up. She looked at once obstinate and weak. Frightened, but trying to hide it. Her expensive clothes were incongruous in this setting; her shoes, though scuffed by coming and going over the rough ground, certainly didn't come from any chainstore. The handbag lying beside her was of real leather, from some very fancy boutique; the diamond on her finger was no imitation.

When they'd got over their surprise – they couldn't have been in the habit of receiving visitors – Bébert spoke.

'What is it?' he asked.

'I don't know if you recognize me,' I answered, 'but here's something to refresh your memory anyway.'

I took a swing at him. He staggered back, fell over a packing case and crashed to the floor. His girl looked on in astonishment. By the time he'd struggled to his feet and begun to square up to me, I'd whipped out my gun. He drew back.

'Hey,' he said, 'what's that?'

'It's a gun, and you're not laughing as hard as you did yesterday, are you? It's not six against one now. You're all on your own, like the big jerk and little twit you really are!'

He tried to protest.

'It's illegal to threaten someone with a gun!'

'Is it really? But it's all right for you to bother people, and then beat up anyone who doesn't appreciate your daft jokes? For your information, I'm a private detective, and you let yourself in for trouble when you got on the wrong side of me.'

They both gasped. The girl stood up, and then sat down again. I pointed the gun at her.

'You stay where you are, too!' I said.

She didn't need telling twice, and curled herself up in a corner like a frightened cat. I whirled round and brought the butt of my gun down on Bébert's hand, which had crept a bit too close for my liking. He gave a howl and started to dance about in pain. I took another almighty swing at him, and he lost his balance and keeled over, sitting down on a packing case that fell to pieces under his weight. I hoped he had a good big splinter in his backside.

Still rubbing his thumped hand, now going all colours of the rainbow, he said: 'OK. You want your revenge. That's reasonable enough. But if you're not satisfied yet, I'd rather we finished this off somewhere else.'

He made as if to get up.

'Don't move,' I said. 'We'll forget my revenge for the moment. I don't want to get my clothes messed up – I'm meeting a client at eight o'clock and I need to be presentable. I really came here to talk.'

'Talk?'

'I ask the questions and you give the answers.'

He shrugged. The crate disintegrated some more.

I pushed another crate over with my foot and sat down facing him. 'Did you know the girl who was with me at the Fair?'

'No. Why?'

'I suspect that fight was a put-up job. Somebody paid you to lay it on.'

'You must be crazy.'

'How can you be reached on the phone? If someone wanted to give you instructions, say. Is there a bar where people can get in touch with you?'

'No. I suppose they could phone me at my hotel. Or at work. But no one ever does.'

'What hotel?'

'The place where I sleep, of course!'

'Don't you sleep here?'

'Well . . . sometimes.'

'And you can also be reached at work. So you've got a job, have you?'

'Yes. I'm a mechanic. Sort of.'

'I thought you were a wrestler.'

'Oh, you know about that, do you? But that was last year. And I wasn't exactly a wrestler – just a stooge. It wasn't a living. So one day I decided I'd better quit and stop playing the fool. Try to, anyway.'

'And as soon as you got a job you ditched your mother, eh?'

'You know about that too?'

'Yes.'

'My mother! . . .' He rolled his eyes, letting out a sound that was half a sarcastic groan and half a sob. Perhaps his being a yob wasn't entirely his own fault. But I wasn't going to shed any tears over him. I needed to be able to see clearly.

'Right. So where is it you work?'

'In a little place in the rue Raoul.'

'Where's that?'

'Near the place Daumesnil. Opposite the rue de la Brèche-aux-Loups.'

'The rue de la Brèche-aux-Loups! Well, well! . . . So, you've got a job, but that doesn't stop you going and acting the goat at the Foire du Trône?'

He sighed. 'It's in the family. My father was like that. My mother too . . .'

'Don't pile on the agony, please!'

I grilled him a bit longer, but by now I was sure the fight hadn't been planned: he and his gang spent their evenings making trouble anyway, either at the Fair or elsewhere.

'You see,' he said, preening himself, 'I'm the leader, and I have to think of my prestige. And I hadn't been around in the evening for a few days.'

He winked, intimating that this was because of the girl.

'So yesterday evening they came and called for me. Pulled my leg about settling down! Said they were going to the Fair to have some fun, and wasn't I coming along? If I wanted to go on being the boss, how could I say no? So I went with them, and then there was that trouble with your girlfriend, and I had to stand up for the albino, didn't I?'

'The incident was closed once. And then you all started following us.'

'The others wouldn't let it drop, especially Ernest, the albino. And what would I have looked like, hanging back?'

'You mean you were like a general marching at the head of his troops just because they told him to?'

'Yes! It can turn out that way sometimes!'

Suddenly I felt utterly ridiculous sitting there with a gun in my hand and going to all this trouble for so little result. My scare on the scenic railway seemed to have addled my brains. I felt like giving Bébert a good clout on the nose out of sheer frustration, and put my gun away so that I wouldn't be tempted. As I did so my fingers encountered the photograph of Lecanut. I brought it out and looked at it. The dead crook seemed to be laughing at me.

'Who's that?' asked Bébert.

I passed it to him. You never can tell.

'Do you know him?'

'No.' He handed it back. He seemed to be telling the truth. 'Can I get up now?'

'If you don't try any tricks.'

We both stood up. But as I stepped back from my packing case I bumped into someone. The girl had come up behind me and was staring transfixed at the photograph.

'Reminds you of someone, does it?' I began.

She started to make a dash for it. I grabbed at her, she pulled her wrists out of my grasp, and as she rushed out of the truck Bébert tripped me up and came at me. I managed to step aside, get out my gun, and give him a thump on the head with the barrel. By this time the girl was running in the direction of my car, towards the boulevard Soult. I yelled to the dwarf to stop her. Two men came out of the shack to see what was going on. Then . . . My God! she gave the dwarf a shove that sent him sprawling in the dust, jumped in the jalopy, and drove off into the blue.

I walked back to the truck, cursing and swearing and giving short shrift to the two men and their questions.

'She's gone and she'll never come back! And it's all your fault!' hissed Bébert, standing in the doorway.

'You'll get another girl.'

'Not one like her!' He started to swear too, clenching his fists. It didn't look as if his hand was hurting him now. I waved him back inside the truck with my gun.

'And now I want some information about the young lady,' I told him.

'Too bad. I don't know anything about her.'

'Hasn't she got a name?'

'She said she was called Christine.'

'Christine what?'

'I don't know.'

'Didn't you look in her bag?'

'I'm not a cop!'

I let that pass and looked around.

'There must have been something important in it – she made sure to take it with her. Now come on – tell me what you can.'

'Fat lot of use that'll be! I told you I don't know anything!'

'I'll be the judge of that. Talk!'

'She's been here for five days. I met her at the Foire du Trône. I was larking about with the lads, and we chivvied her like we did your girl, and at first she told us to clear off, but then she came along with us. And there you are!'

'You mean you allocated her to yourself? You were the boss, so you had the right to sleep with her?'

'Yes. Just a couple of hours after we met. I couldn't

believe it at first, but who was I to argue? I knew they wouldn't let anyone smuggle a girl into their room at my hotel, so we came here.'

I made him give me the name of his hotel.

'The funny thing was,' he went on, 'she wouldn't have gone to a hotel anyway. I made enquiries there the next day, and they said it would be all right to bring her so long as she had the proper papers and we paid extra for the room. But she wouldn't hear of it. Peculiar, eh?'

'Maybe there was something wrong with her papers? Maybe she didn't want the police to know where she was?'

'That did occur to me. But it was none of my business, and I wasn't going to make a fuss and risk losing her. I'll never find another bint like her.' This with a scowl at me.

I reckoned all this must be more or less true. He was too dim to be making it up.

'Probably not,' I agreed. 'Did you notice that ring she was wearing? The genuine article. And her clothes . . .'

'Who do you think she was, then?'

'A poor little rich girl with hot pants, who's seen too many James Dean films and likes to go slumming . . . But there could be another explanation. That photograph seemed to frighten her, and she preferred to run for it rather than explain why . . .'

'It was you who frightened her!'

'Maybe. But there was something about the photograph that upset her too.'

'Who the hell was it of, then?'

'A crook called Lancelin. You may have heard of him. He tried to tip someone off the scenic railway the other day, but he met his match and *he* was the one who bought it.'

'Yes – it was in the papers. The other bloke was a private eye . . . My oath!'

'Yes. Yours truly.'

He looked at me with a bit more respect.

'So did Christine know this bloke in the photo?'

'Perhaps. But she seemed frightened before she saw it, too. Was she usually like that?'

'No. Not at all. Maybe it was your barging in like that—'

'How long have you been living here?'

'This would have been the fifth night.'

'And don't the police ever check up on what's going on in this neighbourhood?'

'The shack's one of the Abbé Pierre's shelters, and the police think we're part of the same set-up.'

'Where did you get the money for the bed and so on?'

He pulled some notes out of his breast pocket and held them out to me. 'It was her money. She made me take it. I didn't want it. I'd rather be rid of it.'

I counted the notes. Sixty thousand francs. It wouldn't buy me a new car, but I'd hold on to it for the moment.

'So she must have had at least a hundred thousand with her?'

'Maybe . . .'

I questioned him some more about the girl, but couldn't get anything out of him. He *had* looked in her handbag, but there weren't any papers in it. God, what a twit. She must be a bit lacking too, to have put up with him. Or else she was hiding from something very terrible . . . For, without knowing it, Bébert had been hiding her.

'Right – there was nothing to identify in her bag,' I repeated. 'So why was she so careful to take it with her?'

'Because of the cash. She must still have had about fifty thou left. Go and ask the cops if you want to know any more – she won't come back here. And it's all your fault!'

'Yours, you mean! If you hadn't gone and played the fool at the Fair again yesterday I'd probably never have come here. But no – you're the boss, so you had to go and join your pals!'

'*They*'d better not show their ugly mugs around here again, either!' growled the love-sick swain.

Perhaps Christine had made him turn over a new leaf. Even dopes like him have the right to be in love. That's what makes it such a great thing.

I had a last look round the truck, but could find nothing useful, and left.

Come to think of it, Bébert might have been grieving about his sixty thousand francs.

10 Surprises

I walked up the avenue Emile-Laurent towards the boulevard Soult. No dwarf in sight. He must have disliked the turn things had taken and gone home to the cour Saint-Charles.

Fancy the crack detective having his car pinched, I mused. And I'd been wrong about Simone Blanchet being behind the gang's attack on me . . . But there was still something fishy about her . . .

Where had she come from in that taxi when I went to her place for the second time yesterday? I cudgelled my brains to remember the details on the Taxito Taxi Company card, then darted into the next café I came to. I had an appointment with M. Charles Montolieu in a quarter of an hour in the avenue de Saint-Mandé, but that could wait.

'Hallo? Taxito Taxi Company?'

'Yes, monsieur.'

'Is the driver of taxi 7501 there, please?'

'I'll find out. Do you want me to send him round?'

'No. I'd just like to speak to him on the phone. I want to ask him something.'

'OK – I'll see.'

The next thing was a confident young voice at the other end. After the preliminaries: 'Do you remember driving a fare, a woman, to the rue de la Bréche-aux-Loups at about seven yesterday evening?'

'That's in the 12th, isn't it?'

'Yes. And the passenger was tall and dark and very pretty. Well dressed, but gives the impression she hasn't any clothes on. I should think you must have noticed.'

'That's right! I did notice – not what you just said, but the woman herself, the address and the time.'

'And where did you pick her up?'

'At Richelieu-Drouot.'

There were some other questions I'd have liked to put to him, but I'd ask them later on. I thanked him, hung up and dialled Bébert's hotel. Yes, he did live there – he rented a room by the month. But he'd been away for two or three days.

I had a quick drink at the bar and headed for my appointment.

It was a large and imposing corner house, with a tower, a veranda, the usual number of doors and windows, and a front garden with a couple of trees in it. One of them stretched a few branches over the wall, as if trying to join its majestic sisters in the street outside. I don't know whether it's anything to do with the fact that the Bois de Vincennes is nearby, but the 12th has more trees in it than any other arrondissement in Paris. I wonder how long *that* will last!

I looked at my watch. Five past eight. I hoped

M. Montolieu wouldn't mind my being late. He must have been watching out for me, because it was he who came and opened the gate when I rang.

He was a man of about fifty, and looked fed up. But then a lot of my clients do. Rather stout; a bit blotchy in the face; with a strong jaw, not much hair, and a sensual nose and mouth. His steely grey eyes went straight into action, sizing me up. If, as I supposed, he was a business man, I wouldn't have liked to be one of his competitors.

He led the way into a luxuriously furnished drawing room on the ground floor. A woman sitting there stood up to be introduced. This was Mme Marthe Montolieu, who looked even glummer than her husband. She was clearly older than he was, and showed her age, but she must have been beautiful once, and still bore herself proudly. She too had a good long look at me . . . But I was forgetting: my face still bore traces of the fracas the other night, and I *had* been mentioned in the papers.

'Can I offer you a glass of wine?' said Montolieu when we were all sitting down. 'I suggest wine because I deal in the stuff – I'm a merchant at Bercy – though the wine I give my friends is better than what I sell!'

The wine was pretty good. I noticed Mme Montolieu didn't have any.

'Well,' said my host and future client, 'I saw your name in the paper and decided to call you in. Extraordinary thing, that business on the scenic railway!'

Another of his piercing looks. When we spoke on the phone he'd said, 'Don't worry. It won't be as

Death of a Marseilles Man

dangerous as the scenic railway.' Did he think I was scared?

'Oh,' I said modestly. 'It was nothing. I'm used to things being out of the ordinary.'

He took a moment to digest that one.

'Well, to get down to serious matters . . . Oh, I'm sorry, I didn't mean . . . It's just that we're so worried . . .'

'That's all right. I quite understand. What is it you're worried about?'

'Our daughter. Or rather my wife's daughter – my stepdaughter. I don't like to criticize—'

He turned to his wife. 'I'm sorry, Marthe, but I think we have to tell this gentleman the truth . . .'

She nodded vaguely. He turned back to me. 'She's a very impulsive girl. Over-imaginative. Full of wild ideas. Likes to have her own way. You may say all young people are like that nowadays, but we think she must really be slightly unbalanced, and we're afraid she might do something foolish.'

He paused as if to give me time to absorb all these shortcomings.

'It seems to me you need a doctor rather than a private detective,' I said.

'We'll take her to a doctor when you've found her,' he answered. 'She's run away from home.'

'How long ago?'

'Five days.'

Small world!

'You left it rather long to start looking for her, didn't you!' I said.

'We weren't really worried at first. We got in touch

88

with all the people we know . . . and the people she knows . . . She might have been staying with one of them. But she wasn't. All that took some time. Then I read in the paper about your excellent reputation, so I thought . . . But that held us up a bit longer, because of the time it took to contact you.'

'What about the police?'

He held up a hand. 'We don't want the police mixed up in all this. If our daughter *has* done anything silly, we want to be able to put matters right without any scandal.'

'I see. Before we go any further, have you got a photograph I could see?'

He was ready for my request, and passed me a picture from an album that was lying on a desk nearby.

No doubt about it. His stepdaughter and Bébert's bint were one and the same.

'Her name's Christine, isn't it?' I said.

They both stared.

'Yes . . . Christine Delay . . . But . . . how did you know?' he gasped.

'I just did. And you're right – she *has* done something foolish. Two things at least. She's got herself into the clutches of a young thug, and she's stolen my car!'

They were dumbstruck.

'I don't understand. . .' he stammered.

'I deserve my reputation, you see!' I laughed. 'I find missing persons even before I'm asked to look for them! True, in this case I've lost her again! . . . The thing was, I had, for reasons of my own, to go and see a young lout who lives in an old railway truck on some waste land, and who should I find with him but a girl called Christine who looks exactly like your daughter! But she was scared of something, and took off in my car.'

Another stunned silence.

'After she ran away from here she went to the Foire du Trône, and it was there she met this youth. Not very bright, but quite good-looking. The James Dean type, if you like that sort of thing. And apparently she does. Anyhow, she went with him to his truck.'

'Do you mean . . . ?' exclaimed Mme Montolieu.

'Yes, madame. They're both very young . . .'

'My God!' She buried her face in her hands.

'And you say she stole your car?' growled Montolieu.

'Yes. She was frightened.'

'What of?'

'I thought you might be able to tell me that.'

I reached into my pocket for the photograph of Lancelin, but the first thing I felt was the money Bébert had handed over. I passed the notes over to the wine merchant, explaining how I came by them. He took them absentmindedly and put them down by the photograph album. Then I gave him the picture of Lancelin.

He gave another start. 'Why did she have this on her?' he cried.

'She didn't. I did. Why, do you know him too?'

'Certainly. Unless it's just an accidental likeness . . .'

'This is only a reconstruction. A photo-fit.'

'But how did it come into your possession?'

'I happen to be interested in the person in question. Who is he? I know him under two names already. Perhaps you know him under a third!'

'Robert Lecanut,' he said.

He got up and took the photo over to his wife.

'It is him, isn't it?'

She nodded. He frowned. 'It's him, right enough,' he said. 'But why on earth are *you* interested in him?'

'All in good time! First of all, can you tell me something about him?'

'Yes . . . But I still don't understand . . . You say Christine got scared when she saw this photograph . . . I don't know why she should have done . . .'

'It might have been my attitude that frightened her. But she did seem very interested in the photo.'

'Perhaps she was like me, and couldn't understand what you were doing with it.'

'Maybe . . . Now, about Lecanut himself, if you don't mind.'

'Well, Delay and I – Delay was Christine's father – were partners. We were old friends – we'd met when we were doing our military service, and then served in the same unit during the war. It was then that we met Lecanut – we were all sent to the same POW camp. We were soon sent off to different work squads, but we got together again after the Liberation, and as Lecanut seemed rather down on his luck Delay offered him a job with us. He did all sorts of things – a bit of selling, a bit of travelling . . .'

'And did he give satisfaction?'

'Certainly. He was more of a friend than an employee. But I still don't see why—'

'You will, in due course. You speak of him in the past tense. Did something happen to him?'

'Not that I know of. But he left the firm in 1952 or '53.'

'And have you seen him since?'

'No. He wrote to us from time to time. From towns in the provinces. He seemed to travel a lot . . . But he never said much. Just "Hope this finds you as it leaves me" sort of thing!'

'Does he still write?'

'We haven't heard from him for two or three years now. That's right, isn't it, Marthe?'

'Yes.'

'Well, you won't be hearing from him again.'

'Why not?'

'He's dead. He was the man on the scenic railway.'

They both cried out in surprise.

Then Montolieu got up and started to pace to and fro. 'But how is that possible? I read the papers . . . I'd have noticed the name!'

'He used several aliases. And the papers referred to him as Lancelin.'

He stood still and rubbed his eyes. 'That's right. And I didn't see any photographs.'

'The ones they took in the morgue weren't presentable.'

Mme Montolieu buried her face in her hands again. 'But I can't understand it . . . Why should he have tried to . . . Were you after him for some reason?'

'He was after me! He wasn't a little plaster saint, you know! When he left your firm, did he just quit or did you fire him?'

'He went of his own accord.'

'With or without part of the till?'

'He was always perfectly honest!'

'Not always. He was involved in some dirty work

recently, and before the war he was gaoled two or three times for theft.'

'We knew nothing about that.'

More pacing about. Then: 'Well, what am I supposed to do about it? As if we didn't have enough trouble already! Do you think I ought to go to the police and tell them I knew the man who attacked you under the name of Lecanut? Roger Lecanut?'

'They know already.'

'What? They know I know him? Knew him, rather?'

'They know his name was Lecanut. And if you haven't met him since 1952 or '53, I don't think your evidence will be of much use. If I were you I'd keep quiet – unless of course the police reveal the name Lecanut to the press . . . Or unless you know of some contacts he had when he worked for you – people he might have kept in touch with.'

'Now you mention it, I realize we never knew very much about him. He always kept himself to himself. Strange how you think you know people, and in fact you know nothing about them at all . . .'

'No women in his life?'

'Yes – he wasn't married, but he did introduce me to a girlfriend once. But whenever he came to dinner he came alone.'

I thought about Simone Blanchet.

What sort of girl? I asked. He couldn't remember, it was so long ago. How long ago? Oh, about seven or eight years. How old was she? About the same age as Lecanut. Could he have met her in the course of his work? At Bercy, perhaps? No, it was definitely not anyone who worked at Bercy.

Forget Simone Blanchet, then.

'I don't think any of this is of any use to the police,' I told him.

'You advise me not to say anything, then?'

'Not unless they mention the name Lecanut.'

'I don't want any trouble . . .'

'There won't be any . . . Now, to get back to our other concerns – that is, to Christine doing a bolt with my car – I think I'd better have a word about it to some of my pals in the police . . . No, don't worry, madame – I'm not going to bring a charge. I'll manage things so as to save face all round, and as your daughter hasn't done anything really seriously wrong yet, there won't be any scandal.'

Of course, thought I, there might, just might, be one little consequence of her shacking up with Bébert. But as good members of the bourgeoisie they wouldn't need any help from me in hushing that up.

I asked if I might use the phone, and got through to Florimond Faroux.

'At last!' he growled.

'Yes, and I'm going to make you laugh! Can you believe it? Someone's to all intents and purposes pinched my car! Of course, it was only a joke—'

'I know. It was stolen by a mysterious girl without any papers who refused to give her name and whom the police haven't yet been able to identify. They've been trying to find you to ask for some explanations. They're waiting for you at the station in the rue due Rendez-Vous. You better get round there at once!'

'I'm on my way!'

'Just a minute! I haven't heard any tall stories for a long time. What's it all about?'

'It's all quite clear and straightforward . . . Hold on
a sec . . .' I covered the mouthpiece and turned to
Montolieu. 'They've found both the car and the driver.
Shall I tell them the truth?'

'Do as you think best,' he said with a sigh.

'My God,' groaned his wife. 'I only hope she hasn't
done anything foolish!'

'Hardly likely, in the time!' Then I spoke into the
phone. 'OK, I'm with you again!'

'Got the story all worked out now?' said Faroux.

'Would I do a thing like that? Now listen. The girl's
name is Christine Delay. I'm with her parents now.
She ran away from home and they asked me to find
her. I did find her, but she slipped through my
fingers . . . nicked my car, just to spite me. But you
say she's at the police station in the rue due Rendez-
Vous now. How come?'

'She had an accident – you can add a bashed-in
mudguard to your bill! I gather she didn't quite know
what she was doing. She hit another car in the place
de la Nation, and was apparently just going to drive on
without stopping when a cop came on the scene. No
identity papers or driving licence. The cop took her to
the station, and there they looked at the car and identified it from the number plates as belonging to you.
They still remembered your name from the other night,
and thought this incident might have something to do
with that scenic-railway business. They rang me, and
I told them to hang on to both the girl and the car until
they could ask you for an explanation. There you are.
Off you go.'

'Right.'

'And *has* it got anything to do with—'

'No.'

I hung up, told Montolieu what Faroux had told me, and asked him if he wanted to come with me to collect Christine.

'I'm coming too,' said his wife.

My car, damaged left wing and all, was standing outside the police station in the rue du Rendez-Vous. Christine was inside, sitting on a bench with her legs crossed, gazing into the void. The youngest of the cops was looking at her legs with interest. Mme Montolieu rushed over and nearly smothered her offspring with kisses, while her husband and I talked to the local super. The reflected glory of Montolieu's social status did something to improve my image with the cops, and before long Christine was restored to the bosom of her family, and I was free to repossess my car.

'My poor naughty little girl,' whimpered Mme Montolieu.

The naughty little girl was sitting defiantly in her parents' drawing-room, her whole attitude proclaiming, 'You may have dragged me back home, but I'll run away again!' It conveyed an even less polite message whenever her eye caught mine.

'But whatever possessed you to run away?' said her mother, oblivious of my presence. 'Aren't you happy here? You've got everything you can possibly want. How could you be so cruel to me?'

'Oh, mother – please!'

Then her mother hugged her, and the girl broke down and started to sob as if she was only about ten years old. An affecting scene . . . Montolieu went over to complete the trio. But he didn't get far. Christine straightened up, her pretty face streaming with tears, her splendid body trembling all over. She stamped her foot. Montolieu drew back.

'Come along, mother,' said the girl. 'I want to go to bed.'

And out they both went.

Montolieu stood rubbing his nose ruefully. 'A step-father's not the same as a real father,' he said.

There was no arguing with that.

'Here—' He picked up the money I'd given him earlier on, and held it out to me. 'Take this.'

'I can't,' I said. 'I only found Christine by accident.'

'Maybe. But she damaged your car. Take it.'

I took it, and tore myself away from that scene of domestic bliss.

11 Queen Christina

But my instincts told me not to go too far. After driving off a little way, I turned round and drove back again, stopping in the shadows almost opposite the Montolieus' house.

It was not quite dark. I sat at the wheel, smoking my pipe and watching the occasional silhouette pass by the lighted windows. I was probably wasting my time. But for the moment I hadn't anything better to do. As I waited I thought. Young Christine was like quicksilver – her mother and stepfather would never be able to hold her. She obviously couldn't bear living there. It wouldn't surprise me if she made another bid for freedom that very night. Of course, if they locked her in . . . But they couldn't lock her in for ever.

Time passed. It was so quiet you could hardly believe you were in Paris. The only sound was the hum of the traffic in the avenue de Saint-Mandé, and there weren't many cars about at this hour.

Suddenly I started. The Montolieus' garage door was sliding open. Their car – a Citroën – emerged. Montolieu got out and banged the garage door shut angrily, not bothering about how much noise he made. Not at all like a husband sneaking off for a night on the tiles. Then he got in the car and roared off. I was prepared to bet he was just going for a drive or a drink to settle his nerves after having a row with his wife about the kid.

More time went by. The lights in the house had all gone out. Everyone in the street was asleep . . . Not quite everyone. A shadowy shape had just slipped out of a little side door near the Montolieus' garage. There was no mistaking that irresistible walk.

It wasn't difficult to overtake her. The sound of the car, quiet as it was, had stopped her in her tracks. I stuck my head out of the window.

'Hey! Chris!' I whispered.

Her hand went to her mouth.

'Ssh! Don't make a noise if you don't want to advertise that you've flown the coop!'

She stared, wide-eyed.

'I was expecting you,' I went on. 'And waiting to give you a hand. Get in and tell me where you want to go.'

She didn't move. Her eyes were back to normal.

'I don't believe it,' she said. 'You've been spying on me. They paid you to find me, and now—'

I put on my most winning smile. 'That's precisely why I want to help you run away! Every time you do it I can get paid for trying to find you! I'll make a fortune!'

She brightened up a little, but still didn't budge.

'Listen, kiddo. Forget what happened this afternoon. The disagreeable part. I'm sorry I was a bit rough with you. We were both taken by surprise over that photograph. But get it into your pretty little head that I don't mean you any harm. Climb in and we'll have a nice little heart-to-heart.'

Still no result.

'Just think about it. If I was being paid to spy on you, would I be sitting here like this chewing the fat? No – I'd just grab you by the arm and haul you back home!'

A sigh. But that was all.

'Maybe you don't know it, but your stepfather has just gone out.'

'I know.'

'He could come back at any minute. If he finds us here together in the street it could be awkward for everyone. And he'll just take you in and lock you up in your room.'

This made up her mind for her, and she got in the car. She didn't know what I had in mind, but apparently she preferred to risk that, whatever it was, rather than face her stepfather.

'Where would you like me to drop you?' I asked, when we'd started up.

'Nowhere.'

'Haven't you anywhere in mind?'

'I was just leaving, that's all.'

'All right – we'll just drive around. Will that suit you?'

She didn't answer. I supposed it did suit her, and started to cruise around the main streets of the 12th arrondissement.

'I've been wanting to have a talk with you,' I said,

'though I didn't like to ask your parents after we got back from the police station. And anyhow I'd rather it was between ourselves. I like you, Chris. You're nice, you're attractive—'

'Are you in love with me?' she said archly.

They're all the same!

'I won't deny it, but I wasn't waiting for you just because of that. All I wanted for now was to have a talk. I think you have problems, and because you're so nice and pretty I'd like to be able to do something for you . . . What's wrong with your home that you're always trying to run away?'

'I feel as if I'm stifling to death there.'

'How long have you felt like that?'

'For as long as I can remember. But it's been worse lately.'

'Why?'

'I don't know. I've felt . . . sort of afraid . . .'

'Of whom? Lecanut?'

That didn't fit chronologically. She'd left home well before Lecanut came back to Paris. But then there was her reaction to the photograph.

'Oh, no!' she said. 'Why should I be afraid of M. Lecanut? I can't say I ever liked him – perhaps I was a bit scared of him. And that might be why I remember what he looks like. But that was a long time ago. There's no reason why I should be afraid of him now. We haven't seen him for years.'

'But you seemed shocked when you saw his photograph?'

'Association of ideas.'

'Explain what you mean, and as a reward I'll tell you

a story. A detective story – I hope you like them. But first tell me about why you acted as you did in the truck, and, while you're about it, why you joined up, even for so short a time, with that young layabout.'

'You don't like him, do you?'

'No, not much.'

'He's not really bad, you know.'

'Yes, he is – it's just that you don't notice at first because he's so stupid!'

'You don't like him,' she repeated. Then she shrugged. 'Liking and not liking – they're just the same. It's all a matter of instinct. But sometimes, later on, you find out you were right . . .'

I told her to skip the philosophy and get down to brass tacks.

'Well,' she said briskly, either deciding she could trust me or wanting to unburden herself, 'I'd run away, and I didn't want them to find me. So I didn't go to any of our friends. I didn't know where to go. I just dropped in at the Foire du Trône to take my mind off things. I hadn't been before, this year. Last year I went nearly every day. And it was there I met those . . . this . . . well, Albert.'

It squared with what the youth himself had said.

'You probably think badly of me,' she said, stammering a little.

'Who am I to judge?'

'I thought I'd be safe with Albert . . . That no one would come and look for me there.'

'And it made you feel a bit like a movie star, too, didn't it? Very different from your usual middle-class background?'

'I suppose so . . . But Albert was nice, too . . .'

'Spare me the details. So what happened when I arrived?'

'When you said you were a private detective I thought my parents had sent you, and that everything you said was just to conceal the fact. And then when you showed me the photograph, that confirmed my suspicions. M. Lecanut was a friend of the family . . . I jumped to conclusions . . . I lost my head . . . and I stole your car. I'm sorry.'

'Forget it!'

'But even while I was driving away I realized I'd behaved like a fool. I didn't know what I was doing. And then I banged into the other car . . .'

'And you wouldn't tell the cops who you were. Was that because you didn't want to go home, too?'

'Yes. I'd rather have gone to prison.'

'You mean you'd have felt safer there? As you did in the truck?'

'Something like that.'

'Listen, Chris,' I said soberly, 'and give me a proper answer this time. What's wrong at home that you'd rather be in an old railway truck, or even in gaol, than there?'

'I'm afraid.'

'But of what? Of whom?'

'I don't know. I can't put it into words. I just feel it . . . Oh God! . . .'

And she suddenly began to weep. I did my best to calm her down, with friendly taps on the shoulder and reassuring phrases. When she was quieter:

'I was told you were wild and impulsive, but I think

you're just exceptionally sensitive. And every now and then, at some times more severely than at others, you experience the after-effects of a trauma dating back several years. It's not unusual. M. Montolieu is your stepfather. And a stepfather isn't the same as a real father. He's noticed it himself. In short, Chris, you don't like your stepfather, and it's him you're afraid of.'

'Do you think so?'

'I'm sure of it.'

'But there's no reason why I should be afraid of him.'

'It isn't a matter of reason. He took over your father's place, your mother's affection. I'd be surprised if you *did* like him!'

'You're right,' she said fiercely. 'I don't like him!'

'And from there it's only a step to being afraid of him. How old were you when your mother remarried?'

'Oh, it was only three years ago! I was just seventeen. I was fifteen when Father died.'

'Were you very fond of him?'

Her voice broke. 'Oh, yes! He was a bad man, but I loved him.'

'How do you mean – a bad man?'

'He was always making Mother cry. And then one day she'd had enough.'

'Had enough?'

What was all this? Was the child insinuating that her mother had done away with her nasty dad? Steady on, Nestor. They told you Chris had wild ideas, but even so . . .

' "Had enough?" I don't quite see—'

'She took a lover.'

Phew, what a relief! Only a lover. Nothing serious. The usual remedy. Maybe the best.

'But my stepfather's often made Mother cry, too. For the same reason. Women.'

Delay and Montolieu were partners. And birds of a feather flock together. What did the ex-widow expect? She and Montolieu had probably only got married for business reasons.

'But I can't forgive my stepfather,' said the girl. 'I'd like to be able to catch him redhanded, but it's impossible.'

Help! She wasn't going to offer me a job tailing him, was she?

'There's no way of finding out who his mistress is. Or mistresses. No one could find that out, even when Father was alive . . .'

She stopped.

'Find out what?' I prompted.

'Even before he married Mother he had other women . . . Even when Father was still there . . . I was too young to understand at the time. But later on I remembered things and realized what they meant. And that's another reason why I dislike him. Why I *hate* him!'

She buried her face in her hands, like her mother, and wept.

'Poor Mother . . . poor Mother . . . I do love *her* . . .'

I left her to relieve her feelings for a bit, then spoke out.

'If you're so fond of her, why do *you* make her cry too, keeping on running away like this? What do you think she's going to feel like when she goes into your room tonight or tomorrow morning and finds the bed empty?'

'But what am I supposed to do? I told you – I'm afraid!'

'Nonsense! Pull yourself together! Nothing's going to happen to you. Unless you go on playing the fool and exhaust your mother's patience, and then she and her husband might take stern measures. Are you still a minor?'

'I'll be of age in five weeks from now. In five weeks' time I shall be queen! Then *I* shall rule the roost!'

I glanced at her. She looked as odd as she sounded. Perhaps she was a bit cracked after all, and her story came partly out of her head. But anyhow I had other fish to fry.

'That's right,' I said. 'You'll be Queen Christina. But meanwhile, just take my advice. Go quietly back home to bed and to sleep. You have nothing to fear – all your terrors are imaginary. If there *should* be anything – though I don't believe for a moment that there will – here's my card, with my address and phone number. And here are two other numbers, belonging to my agents. There's bound to be at least one of us available if you need help. But I'm sure you won't – it's just to make you feel more secure. I have the feeling you need reassurance.'

'Thank you!' she said, with disproportionate gratitude.

Yes, she certainly did have a tendency to exaggerate.

'Right. So shall we go back, then?'

'Yes.'

'Good. And now, because you've been a good, sensible girl and trusted me, I'll tell you the story I promised you. I'm afraid it may give you nightmares, but there are certain things I think you should know.'

But I didn't tell her everything. Just that Lecanut was a gangster (I didn't go into detail), the dirty trick he'd tried to play on me, and how I came to be in possession of his photograph.

'Heavens!' she said. 'I told you I never liked him! And that he scared me somehow . . .'

'Yes, yes. How long ago was it that you last saw him?'

'I told you – years ago. I never saw him again after he left the firm. About a year after Father died.'

'Who was closer to Lecanut, your father or your stepfather?'

'There wasn't any difference. M. Lecanut was friendly with them both.'

I went on trying, but that was all she knew about Lecanut. I stopped the car a short distance away from the house, as before. Everything was quiet.

'I'll drop you here, Mlle Delay, so as not to disturb anyone,' I said. 'I hope you get in safely.'

She climbed out of the car.

'Thank you, monsieur,' she whispered. 'You . . . you've been really nice. I feel better now.'

She held out her hand. I held it in mine for a moment. It was soft and pleasant.

'That's what the girls always say!' I joked.

She leaned closer. 'Goodnight,' she breathed again. 'Goodnight, Chris.'

I watched her move silently towards the house, skipping lightly over the gutter. Perhaps the pretty little creature did have some cause to be frightened after all. Mightn't Montolieu, the womanizer, be all too susceptible to his stepdaughter's charms?

Suddenly I had a curious feeling. A feeling of *déjà vu*. It was as if I seen it all before – Delay, the wine merchant, Christine . . . It was like a dream. The sort of sensation you sometimes get when you're feeling below par. I'd had it the other night, standing under the struts of the scenic railway, when the plain-clothes cops showed up. A sort of mental transposition whereby, instead of seeing them, I saw Grégoire and myself standing among the crowd at the Gare de Lyon . . . It was then, subconsciously, that my theory about Lancelin had begun to take shape . . .

12 The Juice of the Vine

I went back to the office to sleep, nervous as a cat. But badly as I needed rest – I could still feel the effects of the fight, and the real work was only just beginning – I couldn't doze off. The only thing to do was swallow some sleeping pills. I swallowed some sleeping pills.

When the ringing of the phone awoke me next morning, I saw from my watch that it was just after eleven.

'Hallo?'

'Faroux here!' he roared. 'I thought I told you to stay quiet!'

'That's right. What am I supposed to have done?'

'You've dug out a witness who used to know Lecanut, and not only have you failed to inform us of the fact—'

'I haven't had time!'

'Don't give me that! Not only have you failed to inform us of the fact, but you've advised the said witness not to come forward himself. Don't try to tell me you meant to give us a surprise! Fortunately the person in question is a bit more public-spirited than you are. Not that his evidence tells us anything, but at least he did come in and make a statement. You know who I'm talking about?'

I sighed. 'A wine merchant called Montolieu, I suppose,' I said.

'Yes. That bothers you, doesn't it?'

'No. It'd take more than that.'

'What about that sigh, then?'

'I've got a hangover. Do we have to ask the cops for permission to sigh now? Anyhow, what's all the fuss about? You say yourself Montolieu hasn't got any useful evidence to spill.'

'Not as such, but he gave us the names of some people Lecanut used to know when he worked at Bercy, and who may have kept in touch with him.'

'You don't meant to say you think—' I began sardonically.

'That'll do! I didn't ring you up to ask you for your opinion! I rang you up to tell you off and remind you to keep your nose out of this damn case!'

Bang!

And the same to you! Only I didn't bang my receiver down quite so loudly as he did. I was still feeling a bit fragile.

I started to shave. My reflection in the mirror looked about as intelligent as Bébert. The phone rang again. This time it was the wine merchant himself.

'I suppose it wasn't quite the thing,' he stammered. 'I really ought to have let you know that on reflection I couldn't follow your advice about keeping quiet. At the time . . . but when I thought about it afterwards . . . So this morning . . .'

'I know. You went and told the police you used to

know Lecanut. I've just had a dressing-down from Superintendent Faroux.'

'I'm sorry. But you do understand my position . . .'

'Of course. Duty must come first. Let's say no more about it.'

'Are you angry?'

'No. I said let's forget it . . . Or rather, just one more word. You told Superintendent Faroux about some people Lecanut knew when he worked at Bercy. You might have told *me*. I'm interested too.'

'I did mention it! If you'd asked for their names I'd have given them to you!'

'Yes – you're quite right. I'm sorry. I'm not being fair. It's the effects of that dressing-down.'

'Don't apologize. But good Lord, why are they making all this hullabaloo about Lecanut? Of course, he did try to kill you . . .'

'But that's not all.'

'What else?'

'Didn't the cops tell you?'

'No.'

'In that case I can't either. A trade secret . . . Apart from all that, how's Christine?'

'Very well, thank you.'

'You know she doesn't like you?'

'Er . . . You're very quick on the uptake. M. Burma!' The usual starchiness, but underneath he was angry.

'Not always. I was thinking about it just before you rang, and I don't feel very proud of myself on that score. But to get back to Christine – you ought to send her to stay with friends or relations in the country.

Friends or relations of her own. Otherwise she'll run away again, and you'll have to keep running after her. It's your physical presence she can't stand.'

'Really, monsieur – you go too far.'

Now he was furious and no mistake.

'I'm sorry. That dressing-down keeps repeating on me.'

He cooled down a bit. 'Forgive me. That was all my fault. As for Christine . . . yes, you're right. I only wish you weren't . . .'

'Remember me to her. And say if I'm ever in the neighbourhood . . .'

'You'll always be most welcome, M. Burma.'

And that was that. I filled my pipe, lit it, and fixed myself a drink by way of breakfast. Then I lay down, smoking, drinking and thinking.

After a while I reached for the phone.

'Is that the Taxito Taxi Company?'

'Yes, monsieur.' The shrill voice of a boy.

'The Fiat Lux Agency here – rue des Petits-Champs. I'd like a cab. Number 7501.'

'Number 7501? Hold on a minute . . .' He must have gone and consulted a list. 'It's out at the moment. We could send you—'

'No, I'll wait. When will it be back?'

'Any moment now.'

'Well, send it along as soon as possible. Have you got the address?'

'Yes, thanks, inspector!'

'And no tricks, do you hear? I want that cab and I want that driver.'

'But the 7501's usual driver isn't in today.'

My hand tightened round the receiver. 'Has something happened to him?'

'No. He just isn't here today.'

'I see – it's his day off.'

'No. He just didn't show up.'

'Oh . . . Now listen, my boy, I like the sound of you. "Yes, thanks, inspector"! – I bet you're a mystery fan!'

'Sure thing!'

'Well, take down this number, buddy' – he did so, – 'and as soon as the 7501's usual driver comes in . . . What's his name, by the way?'

'Just a mo while I look . . .' Loud clatter as he threw the phone down. Scrape as he picked it up. 'Elie Grainard, monsieur.'

'Right. Well, the minute Grainard shows up, tomorrow or the day after, no matter when, you give me a ring on this number and send him off to this address. Got it?'

'Yeah, man!'

Then I called up the Henri-Marc Wine Company at Bercy.

'She's not here. She didn't come in to work today, monsieur.'

Everyone seemed to be skiving off today. I had another drink and went out for lunch, calling in on the way to consult a couple of friends of mine who are knowledgeable about locks and keys. But they couldn't help me about the key Lecanut had lost in the course of our aerobatics: the fancy handle didn't mean anything to them. Oh well, an interesting souvenir.

After lunch I pointed the car, its wing still dented,

in the direction of the rue de la Brèche-aux-Loups: Simone Blanchet might be at home since she wasn't at work. But she wasn't at home either. Never mind; there was no shortage of girls these days. I'd try Christine.

In the avenue de Saint-Mandé, it was Christine herself who greeted me. So she hadn't run away again – I'd soon start thinking women took my advice. I had a good look at her. Her eyes still showed a trace of fear, but less than before.

'I was passing by,' I said, 'and I had an hour or so to spare. So I thought . . .'

'How kind!'

She ushered me into the drawing-room, where her mother was working gloomily at some sort of tapestry. After presenting my respects to the Penelope of the plonk, and enquiring after the health of her husband (as if I cared) – he was quite well, thank you very much, and at his office in Bercy – I asked if I might take Christine out for a spin.

'Where would you like to go?' I asked her when we were out in the car.

She smiled. 'To the zoo!'

As we drove there – I took the long way round to avoid going anywhere near Bébert's truck – I asked her if she'd got back into the house safely the other night.

'Your mother didn't notice anything?'

'I don't think so.'

'What about your stepfather?'

'He came in a long time after me. But I was still awake, so I heard him.'

'I gave him some advice about you when we were talking on the phone . . .'

'I know. He mentioned it over lunch. I think I'll be going away, a couple of days from now, to stay with some cousins of my father's in the south of France.'

'Good.'

After feeding the elephant and guffawing with the rest of the crowd at some monkeys quarrelling over an old bra, we sat outside the zoo café, watching a camel stalk by with a cargo of apprehensive infants.

'I suppose that when you said you'd be a queen in five weeks' time,' I said, 'you meant that that's when you come of age and inherit your father's business.'

'Yes. It's in Father's will.'

'And what will become of your stepfather? Will you sack him when you succeed to the throne?'

'I'd like to . . . I don't know if I can, though, unless I buy him out . . . But even if he's still a partner, he won't have things all his own way any more.'

'But you will.'

'I, or someone I appoint in my stead. And I'll make sure it's someone who takes his orders only from me! My stepfather will have to know his place.'

'Bravo!' I laughed. 'Though I must say I can't see you beavering away among the barrels at Bercy!'

She shook her auburn hair, and was suddenly grave. 'You'll never see me among the barrels at Bercy,' she said. 'Never!'

'Why not?'

'I can't bear the place!'

'Don't like the smell, eh?'

'It's not that,' she answered. 'It's the memories. It was there that my father died.'

'Oh? He died suddenly, did he? Well, at least he didn't suffer, then . . .'

'Yes, he did . . .'

Her eyes filled with tears. 'He was drowned. In an accident . . . Please don't ask any questions. It's too painful to talk about . . .'

She stood up. 'Let's go, shall we?'

She gave me a piteous smile. 'You're not cross with me, are you?'

'What an idea!'

She clutched my hand. 'You *are* kind! . . . To think I was afraid of you yesterday . . . when really you're so sympathetic and understanding . . .'

'I should hope so!' I said.

After taking Christine home I drove on to the wine depôt at Bercy – a small city in itself – and parked outside. The man at the gate directed me to the premises of Delay and Montolieu, and I made my way there through the rows of narrow streets named after famous vintages and lined with low wooden buildings, past all the sights and sounds of the glorious trade, not to mention the smells. The trees, some of them said to have been planted by Le Nôtre in the seventeenth century, seemed unaffected by the atmosphere.

The small building that housed the offices of Delay and Montolieu was in need of a coat of paint. Behind it were masses of barrels, tuns and casks of all sizes. Two huge cylindrical tanker wagons stood idle, as if abandoned, in a sort of drive. The single name 'Delay', which must once have stood out boldly on their sides, was now almost illegible.

Charles Montolieu, hat on head and pigskin gloves in hand, was surprised to see me.

'To what do I owe the pleasure?' he cried. 'If you'd come five minutes later you'd have missed me. What can I do for you?'

'I've come for my compensation. You got me into hot water with the cops. Their complaints have given me a thirst. I'm here to cadge a few bottles of wine.'

'Very well,' he sighed. 'White or red?'

'Both. And I wouldn't say no to some rosé.'

'I'll get them to make a selection.'

He sent someone to get the wine, and meanwhile looked at his watch.

'I'm afraid I have to go. Please forgive me.'

We shook hands.

'I'm awfully sorry about going to the police. I'd no idea—' he began.

'That's OK. I mean to forget all about it – with the aid of your nectar!'

He left, and so, a little while later, did I, three bottles under each arm. But before leaving the premises I spotted an elderly workman standing in a doorway.

'Excuse me,' I said. 'M. Montolieu has just made me a present of this wine. But I'm no expert. Is it any good?'

He examined the bottles carefully. 'Excellent,' he said, looking at me no less intently.

'Many thanks! Have you been working for Delay and Montolieu long?'

'Thirty years.'

Another scrutiny. 'You're one of them too, aren't you?' he said.

'One of what?'

'The police, of course!'

'No, I'm not a cop. Are some of them around?'

'Yes. After a bloke called Lecanut who used to work here. I knew him, but he didn't have anything to do with ordinary labourers like me. Would hardly give us the time of day. He was a pal of the bosses – they'd been in the army and the camps together. He left here in '53 or thereabouts, and by all accounts became a gangster. I don't know anything about it. And so I told the two inspectors. If you're a cop as well, that makes three!'

'I'm not a cop, but that doesn't prevent me from being interested in what goes on. Were you working here when M. Delay had his accident?'

'I certainly was!'

'I think it was in . . .'

'Nineteen-fifty-two. October 1952.'

'How did it happen? He was drowned, wasn't he?'

'Yes. In a vat. A very suitable end for a wine merchant, if you ask me! I couldn't face a glass for a week! What happened was, he leaned too far over the vat, was overcome by the fumes, and fell in. He was alone and it was at night – he'd stayed on late to finish some work – so they didn't find him till the morning. Nothing to be done by then.'

13 Where Simone Had Been

'Is that you, Chris?'

'Yes.'

'Nestor Burma speaking.'

'Good evening.'

'I'm calling you about that trip we were talking about. I've been thinking. You've been going through a bad patch – it would do you good to have a change. So go as soon as you can.'

'It's all settled. I'm leaving in a matter of days. Perhaps hours.'

'The sooner the better.'

'Is that all you wanted to say?'

'Yes. Goodnight, Chris.'

After I'd put the receiver down I stood there with my hands still resting on it, repeating to myself: 'Goodnight, Chris.'

Fool that I was . . .

Then I had a drink and a smoke, and pondered.

Florimond Faroux was the only person who could help me, but I didn't want to ask him. He was always bawling me out for operating independently: I might as well give him something to grumble about. Anyhow, I couldn't act yet, and in the meantime I might find a way either to make use of Faroux without causing a row, or else to manage without him.

I looked at my watch. Twenty past ten. Never too late . . . I filled another pipe, had another drink, and left the office. Once more into the breach. Once more to the rue de la Bréche-aux-Loups.

The whole building seemed to be asleep. I went up to Simone's floor and knocked at the door. Not a sound. I tried the lock, but found there was a bolt as well. I gave up.

An hour later I came back and had another go. Same result. I went and sat out in the car, waiting for her to come home from the cinema. If she'd gone to the cinema. It was about the time when the evening performance usually ends, and sure enough a few people soon appeared in the street, straggling home to bed. Then the last doors shut, the last lights went out, and a drunk could be heard singing near by. But still no Simone.

At one o'clock I went home to bed too.

Christine was taking part in a radio game where she had to stand on a very insecure plank over a huge vat of wine swarming with horrid corpses. When a bell rang, said the presenter, Christine would be thrown into the vat. A bell did ring somewhere, and I started forward to save her . . .

I came to beside my bed with the telephone shrilling.

'Is that the Fiat Lux Agency?' said a hollow voice.

'Nestor Burma, the director, speaking.'

'This is Philip Marlowe . . .'

I wasn't in the mood for jokes, and treated my caller to a volley of oaths that were all the stronger for having enjoyed a night's rest.

'Hey, hey!' said the voice. 'Don't you remember? Philip Marlowe – Raymond Chandler!'

'I see! You're the Taxito Agency, I presume?'

'That's right! Well, Grainard's here!'

'Great! Buzz him along, kiddo!'

It was half-past six. I didn't know if the day had begun well, but at least it had begun early.

The cab, with 'Taxito' blazoned on the door, drew up beside me. I'd gone down to wait for it outside. The driver was a young fellow with bleary eyes and the general appearance of one who's been on the booze. He'd shaved himself with none too steady a hand, and given up on one cheek altogether.

'I'm the client who phoned for a taxi,' I told him. 'But if you'd like to come upstairs for a minute first, I've got something for you. You won't regret it.'

Back in the office I gave him a hair of the dog. He stood and knocked back the whisky in one gulp.

'So what is it you've got for me?' he asked.

'A punch on the nose or some cash – it's up to you. I shouldn't really give you the choice. I don't like third-rate drunks trying to lead me up the garden. Sit down, Grainard.'

He did so. 'So you know my name?'

'Yes, and I also know that if you played hookey yesterday and went on the razzle, it was because you'd been paid by someone for doing something. You got the money by post – sent by a tall and beautiful brunette who gives the impression that she hasn't got any clothes on. The woman I described to you over the phone three days ago.'

'Oh, I begin to see,' mumbled Grainard.

'Good. You drove her to the rue de la Brèche-aux-Loups, and I want to know where you picked her up. Over the phone you told me Richelieu-Drouot. Rubbish. I could tell at once you were making it up. You're a rotten actor.'

He shrugged. 'I was just doing what she asked, and saying what she told me to say if anyone asked that sort of question. I went along with it because she was such a good-looker – even on the phone she could stir you up . . .'

'She gave you your instructions by telephone, did she? That must have been early in the morning on the day after you'd driven her home.'

'You know everything, don't you!'

'A little bolt told me.'

Yes, a bolt. I'd seen Simone drawing it the night I slept at her place. But next morning the door was unbolted. So Simone must have slipped out early without my knowing, and as it wasn't to buy milk and croissants – we'd had only black coffee for breakfast – it must have been on some other errand. This had added to my previous suspicions.

'So what was it she said to you on the phone?'

'She said some bloke was bothering her about where she'd taken the taxi, and he knew the name of the firm because he'd seen the card, and if he rang up and asked me I was to say I picked her up somewhere in the middle of town. It was a question of protecting her reputation . . . So I said OK, and she asked me my name and address and sent me five ten-franc notes.'

'And where *did* you pick her up, really?'

'At Saint-Mandé. In a street where I'd never have expected to find a fare. I was just cruising.'

'H'm . . . funny idea, that – cruising in a place where you didn't expect to pick up any clients . . .'

'I'd had to go a long way round to get back to Paris because of some road works, and I just happened to be in that street.'

'Which street?'

'I don't know.'

'But you'd recognize it?'

'Yes.'

'Let's go.'

'This is it,' said Grainard.

The rue Louis-Lenormand had houses on one side and open ground on the other, with the inevitable building site at one end.

'Yes,' he went on. 'And I wouldn't swear to it, but I think she'd just come out of one of those houses over there.'

He pointed to a couple of villas standing at some distance from one another in about the middle of the street.

'Right,' said I. 'Drive on past them and stop a bit further down.'

He did so. I got out and walked back. The first house was obviously lived in, but the second seemed temporarily empty. It was an ordinary-looking place, with a first floor and above that quite a large attic. The upstairs shutters were open, but the white-curtained windows were closed. The front garden had two fine chestnut trees growing in it, and an ivy-covered wall shutting it off from the street.

I puffed at my pipe. Of course there was no actual proof that this was where Simone had come from. But if she'd taken the precaution of trying to cover her tracks, it must have been because if I found out where the cab-driver had picked her up I'd know ipso facto where she'd been. Ergo: she'd probably been to this second house.

The front gate – double-locked – was an iron grille. I had a look through the bars at the garden. Part of it was lawn, but some of it was stony, barren-looking earth, one patch of it covered with a tarpaulin held down at the corners with pebbles. The ground-floor shutters were closed.

The gateposts gave no indication of the name of the house or of its owner. I pulled the bell and heard it jangling inside the house, but no one came.

I went on puffing at my pipe. Simone must have come here between the two visits I paid to her place the other day. To report on our first interview, or to receive instructions. There ought to be some useful clues inside the house.

I looked up and down the street. No one about, except Grainard in his taxi, no doubt keeping an eye on me through the rear window. Seven-twenty a.m., and all's well. No sign of activity from the other house. The ivy would help me over the wall. I'd already reached up to get a grip on it when I had an idea. I felt my pockets to see if I had Lecanut's bunch of keys on me . . . Yes, I had. I selected the large key with the fancy handle, inserted it into the lock on the gate, and tried to turn it. It worked! It turned! Not even a creak!

I shut the gate behind me. If there was anyone in the house, it was now that they would challenge me. But nothing. The place seemed deserted. I walked up to the front door. Locked. But it yielded to one of the other keys on the bunch. I went in, put my pipe away, and began to search, taking care not to leave any traces.

The kitchen was clean and rarely used; the drawing-room nicely furnished, clean enough, and clearly not often occupied. But the bedroom – that was something different. Voluptuous indirect lighting. Air heavy with perfume. Soft velvet curtains drawn over shuttered windows. A cosy love-nest equipped with a sumptuous bed in piquant disorder; a wardrobe full of exciting lingerie; and a huge mirror on the wall, flanked by erotic engravings. Whoever would have thought it, looking at the house from outside?

Now the first floor. This had been rather neglected. I neglected it too.

Back in the bedroom downstairs I noticed that something was missing. There didn't seem to be any bathroom. Then I found it, concealed behind a door covered with the same paper as the walls. It wasn't very big, and there was hardly any light from the tiny slit of a window. I found a switch: that was better. A charming bathroom to match the charming bedroom. Complete with washbasin, bidet, WC and bath.

She was in the bath. Her pretty legs were as shapely

as ever, but there was nothing left of her pretty face.

I was overcome with nausea. A good thing I was in a bathroom . . .

When I'd finished heaving my heart up I bent over the body.

It was as stiff as a plank. Death must have taken place more than twenty-four hours ago. Despite the savage attack on the face, it was definitely Simone Blanchet. She was wearing the same blue dress as she'd worn the other evening on the scenic railway, though now it was in shreds and spattered with blood. It looked as if it had been torn in a struggle – unless it had been destroyed afterwards. This was no neat and tidy murder: it was a frightful act of butchery, carried out in a paroxysm of rage. The dead woman's neck bore the brownish traces of strangulation, which seemed to be the cause of death. But the murderer seemed to have attacked the body afterwards with some blunt instrument, either because he hadn't intended to kill Simone and was furious at finding himself with a corpse on his hands, or because he thought mere death was too good for her.

I wondered what Simone could have done to deserve such treatment. She must have done something foolish, made a mistake that somebody found unendurable. But death's no excuse, as Jean Vallès said. Nor is it a guarantee of innocence. Simone's murder, together with the fact that she was in the habit of visiting a house to which Lecanut had the keys, seemed to prove she'd played an active part in all this imbroglio.

A final look round revealed a bedside rug rolled up

in a corner of the bathroom. It might have been covered in blood; I didn't bother to check. Under the washbasin lay a heavy bronze ashtray. Clearly the weapon with which the killer had battered the victim's head. I didn't touch it.

I turned the light off, shut the door and stepped back into the bedroom. It struck me quite differently now. The rumpled bedclothes conveyed a more sinister message: when I straightened them out they proved to be covered in blood. I rearranged them more or less as they were before, and had another look round.

In a cupboard I found a suitcase containing some men's underwear: the labels showed it had been bought in a shop in Marseilles. No doubt this was Lecanut's luggage. Not that that told me much. No point in hanging around. I had the keys and could always come back if I felt like it. Having removed all evidence of my visit, I left.

Out in the garden I lifted one corner of the tarpaulin: underneath were the beginnings of a sinister-shaped hole, some stones turned up in the process of making it, and an amateur gravedigger's tools. The killer, whoever he might be, was a strange character. Fancy choosing to bury Simone's body in ground so hard and full of stones. He must be crazy. Of course, all murderers are a bit mad. But this one must be completely off his rocker.

14 *A Night in Saint-Mandé*

I got into the cab and told Grainard to drive me back to the office. There I paid him handsomely, and he gave me a knowing grin and disappeared out of my life.

Then I drove myself back to Saint-Mandé. I now had a choice between trying to find out more about the murderer and waiting in his house for him to come home. Too easy.

I tried the bell again in case he'd returned while I was away: that would have simplified matters. But again there was no answer.

I called at the other villa. The lady of the house was incapable of describing her neighbour, and didn't know his name. She hadn't lived there long and had never actually seen him. She thought he came there mainly at night, and not regularly even then. She didn't know anything about the digging in the garden, either: he must have done it at night, and quite recently too. The only useful information I got out of her was that his house might be managed by the same agents as her own: the Bonchamps Estate Agency in the avenue Ledru-Rollin.

And since the more I could find out about him before we met, the better . . .

But getting information out of the clerk at the Estate Agency was like getting blood out of a stone. (Ugh!)

'A villa in the rue Louis-Lenormand at Saint-Mandé, with a couple of chestnut trees in the garden? Yes, we do look after it, but it's not our practice to give information about our tenants. The place belongs to a Mme Parmentier – if *she* was willing to tell you anything . . . But I'm afraid *we* can't help you . . .'

I'd have liked to see the look on his face if I'd told him what was in the bathroom of his precious villa.

'And where might I get in touch with Mme Parmentier?'

He grudgingly gave me an address in the boulevard Poniatowski.

Mme Parmentier was a widow of about seventy-five, thin as a rake. But the eyes behind those owlish round horn-rimmed spectacles were bright and youthful. She was dressed in odds and ends, but this was clearly due to eccentricity rather than poverty or avarice: her apartment might have been furnished in a more up-to-date manner, but not more expensively.

When I showed up there, just after midday, Mme Parmentier was having her lunch, attended by a maid not much younger than herself, and the old girl certainly wasn't on a diet. She greeted me without any fuss, and went on with her meal. I took to her at once. There was a lurid detective story open beside her plate, and others lay on a nearby chair, together with a packet of Gauloises. An ashtray full of cigarette ends stood out against the embroidered tablecloth, not far from a bottle of burgundy.

I'd told the maid, when she opened the door, that I'd come about the house in Saint-Mandé, but I'd given an assumed name and refrained from going into detail. However, I could see that Mme Parmentier, unlike the costive clerk at the estate agents', was someone with whom you could speak freely.

When I came out with who I really was she positively quivered with delight, setting her jet earrings a-jangle, and offered me a glass of her excellent burgundy. I told her I was after some information about her tenant in Saint-Mandé.

'His name, for instance, and what he looks like. I don't know anything about him, and I need to know more in connection with a case I'm working on.'

Her eyes sparkled. 'Why, is he mixed up in something?'

I smiled. 'The people private eyes are interested in aren't necessarily mixed up in things that are disreputable. I'm sorry I can't tell you more for the moment, but when the time comes I'll gladly come and tell you everything!'

'I do hope so!' she burbled on excitedly. 'And that it won't be in proportion to what I tell you, because I doubt if I can be of much use to you. I know my tenant's name is Roussel, but I've never met him. The agent sees to all that. The clerk you saw is no good – you need to talk to Bonchamps himself. He bought the agency from Fromentel years ago – I can't remember how long exactly . . . Fromentel's the one who dealt with Roussel originally. Anyhow Bonchamps is away at the moment . . . However, if it can wait that long I'll have a word with him when he gets back – after all, I have the right to know something about my tenant if I choose, haven't I?'

I tried to stem the flood. 'Perhaps I could try to talk to Fromentel in the meanwhile, if he's the one who actually knows Roussel?'

'Fromentel can't help you!'

'Why not?'

'He's dead.'

She said it with relish, like a character out of Agatha Christie . . . As if Fromentel had been cut up in small pieces, and the bits sent round to his friends and relations as birthday presents.

But I hadn't the heart to spoil the old girl's fun.

'Did he die a natural death?' I breathed.

'Yes,' she said with a sigh, just managing to refrain from adding 'Unfortunately!'

And so it went on. But although we chatted away until four o'clock, and Mme Parmentier enjoyed herself hugely, I didn't get any further with my enquiries. When at last I made my escape, my sprightly hostess saw me out, straight as a ramrod, light as a feather, nimble as a goat, with yet another cigarette dangling from the corner of her mouth.

'I'll see Bonchamps and get in touch,' she promised. 'Isn't it fascinating!'

What was she going to say when she found out that her respectable family villa had served as an abattoir?

No need to worry. Her boring little agents might be horrified, but the aged mystery addict would be over the moon.

Back in Saint-Mandé the situation was unchanged. No one there except the corpse. I drove back into Paris and had a quick snack at the counter of a café. Then to the office, intending to have a rest in preparation for what looked like being an eventful night. I set the alarm for eight o'clock, stretched out on the bed, and was woken some time later by the phone.

I recognized the voice at once.

'Hallo, Chris!'

'It's all arranged! I'm off tomorrow afternoon, on the Mistral! I wanted you to know . . . It was partly your idea . . .'

'Good! I'm very glad!'

'Will you come and see me off at the Gare de Lyon?'

'What time is the train?'

'Ten past one.'

'I'll try to come. Is M. Montolieu there?'

'He's at Bercy.'

'I shan't disturb him, then. I only wanted to thank him for some bottles of wine that he gave me yesterday. Will you give him the message if you get the chance?'

'I'll ask my mother to.'

'Right 'Bye, Chris.'

'See you tomorrow!'

I looked out of the window at an overcast sky, disconnected the phone and went back to sleep.

A distant clock struck midnight. It was pitch dark in

the godforsaken rue Louis-Lenormand, which wasn't yet provided with modern streetlamps. No moon, either, because of the clouds.

I'd let myself into the house at about nine, just before it started to rain: a fine drizzle which occasionally lashed against the window where I stood looking out towards the chestnut trees, and which was no doubt forming a pool in the tarpaulin over the unfinished grave. A leaky gutter dripped monotonously somewhere.

Three hours I'd been waiting now. The murderer couldn't just leave things as they were. He'd have to come back and finish the job. But probably not in this lousy weather.

I went on waiting anyhow. I was in a room on the first floor, from which if it hadn't been so dark I'd have had a good view of the garden and the gate. I'd perched myself on the arm of a chair with my gun within reach. The rain plashed down. A dog barked far away. The old furniture let out an occasional creak. I went on waiting. For Simone's murderer. For Lecanut's accomplice.

I swore. My way of greeting rosy-fingered dawn. Uncomfortable as my point of vantage was, I'd somehow dozed off, and now it was starting to get light. I looked at my watch. Nearly five o'clock. It had stopped raining, but everything was drenched. Yes, there was a little pool in the middle of the tarpaulin. So no one could have come and touched it while I was asleep.

It looked like being a fine day. Maybe it wouldn't rain tonight, and my quarry would come back. I'd come back myself as often as I had to. I picked up my gun, put the chair back where I'd found it, looked round to see there were no other traces to clear up, and started to go.

At the bottom of the stairs I froze. Someone *had* been here while I was asleep. There were damp muddy footprints clearly visible in the hall. And lying on the floor by the bedroom door was some sort of cloth or towel that hadn't been there last night.

Yes, someone had come. And perhaps that someone was still there.

I took out my gun and listened. Not a sound. I slipped quietly into the drawing-room. Empty. So was the kitchen. Before checking the love-nest I picked up the cloth by the door: it turned out to be a pair of men's underpants from among Lecanut's things. The label said 'Bini, rue Vacon, Marseilles'. I tossed the pants aside and went in. Empty. Whoever it was must have come and then gone away again. I was lucky he hadn't come upstairs, found me asleep, and bumped me off. Next time I must take something to keep me awake.

Meanwhile, what had the visitor come here for in the pouring rain? Hell – he hadn't taken the body away, had he?

I rushed into the bathroom. No, Simone was still there. The smell was growing noticeable. As I hastily shut the bathroom door I noticed Lecanut's case in a corner of the bedroom – open, ransacked, torn apart, the tartan lining ripped to pieces like Simone's dress. But this time the vandal wasn't only venting his fury. He'd suddenly thought the house might contain a secret hiding place, and had come in the night, despite the rain, to search for it. But what was he looking for? And had he found it? I didn't know, and I wasn't going to find out by hanging around. Nor by going anywhere else, for that matter.

I left everything as it was and let myself out of the house, locking up behind me. I'd parked the car about a kilometre away. Back home, I set the alarm for eleven, disconnected the phone, and went to bed. The crack detective had a new system, specially invented for the present case, which involved spending most of his time asleep.

15 The Wine is Drawn

The alarm didn't go off, and by the time I woke up Chris's train was already past Fontainbleau. I reconnected the phone and rang Montolieu to apologize for not managing to get to the station. He said Christine had been disappointed when I didn't turn up on the platform, and we both hung up, hoping that in spite of this contretemps she'd have a good trip.

Now what was I going to do to pass the time?

There was nothing of interest in the papers. Faroux still hadn't let on that Troyenny, the fire-eater, had been arrested. No mention of the investigations at Bercy among Lecanut's former colleagues. I scanned every paragraph, but neither Simone Blanchet's employers nor her neighbours had reported that she was missing.

At last it was time to go on duty again at Saint-Mandé. It was a magnificent clear night, just right for a spot of digging. This time I took precautions: in the course of a hearty dinner I took some pep-pills that would have made Martine Carole seem like a sedative. Again I left the car some distance away from the rue Louis-Lenormand. Inside the house all seemed to be as I'd left it. No one had been back since last night. I settled down to wait.

He came at about eleven. On foot. He didn't make any noise, nor did the gate, but it was a bright starry night and from my look-out post on the first floor I could see the figure of a man, even if I couldn't distinguish his features. I drew back instinctively from the window, but he didn't look up; he didn't suspect he was being watched.

I crept to the top of the stairs and listened. I heard the visitor come in through the front door – which he shut but didn't lock behind him – switch on some lights, then come and go in the drawing-room, moving the furniture around as if he was doing some spring-cleaning. I went down the stairs, gun in hand, to a point where I could see him without being seen. The man came out of the drawing-room and headed for the bedroom. M. Roussel evidently felt quite at home. Cool as a cucumber. He was fairly stout, and his hair, moustache and suit were all dark. His horn-rimmed spectacles, rather like those Mme Parmentier wore, caught a faint gleam of light from the lamp in the hall. When he saw the underpants still lying where I'd left them, he picked them up without showing any sign of surprise and took them with him into the bedroom. Perhaps this was part of his general tidying up.

I went down and had a squint through the half-open door. The sound of a chain being pulled indicated that he was now in the bathroom. This was the moment to go and ask him what the body was doing in the bath, and why he didn't yell when he saw it. If I confronted him anywhere else he might say he didn't know anything about it.

I tiptoed across the room, noticing as I did so that the battered suitcase had disappeared, presumably put away by the tidier-up. I could see the good housekeeper himself from behind, leaning over the bath and trying to wrap the body in a blanket.

'OK, Roussel,' I said. 'That'll do. She can't do you any more harm now.'

He let go, and Simone's head banged grimly against the edge of the bath. He nearly hit the ceiling.

'Hands up!' I barked. 'And quick!'

He obeyed, his steely grey eyes glittering with fury behind his specs, his strong jaw jutting dangerously.

'Nestor Burma!' he hissed.

And then his fury got the better of him again. He swore horribly at the dead woman, and kicked at her arm as it dangled over the side of the bath, like Marat's after Charlotte Corday had finished with him. Now I knew for sure why he'd killed her. I sprang forward, grabbed him by his well-cut lapels, and shook him. His glasses flew off and broke. It didn't matter – he could see as well as I could. Not just for the moment, though, because I socked him on the head with the barrel of my gun and he fell back, half-unconscious, on the corpse. I bound him hand and foot with the aid of a towel and his own belt, dragged him out into the drawing-room, and slung him into a chair like a bag of dirty washing. In the course of the proceedings his hairpiece got dislodged. I put it back more or less in place.

There was a bottle of wine and a glass on the sideboard: my friend here had no doubt been having a drink to summon up his courage. I opened the sideboard and treated myself to a special round. Now for my clairvoyant act, after which, if there was any justice in this world, I would be in line for the reward offered by the Paris Precious Metals Consortium.

I put my pistol down, drew up a chair and began.

'Well, Montolieu? (Let's forget about Roussel – that was only for the estate agents, wasn't it?).'

He glared at me and said nothing.

'The wine is drawn. Now you have to drink it . . . I know where the gold is, you see! There was a moment when you had me flummoxed – when you went and told the police you knew Lecanut. Then I realized that since they'd have found out anyway, your giving them a statement and saying I'd advised you not to was a way of getting them on my back instead of yours. Unfortunately for you, Faroux only blew me up, and I was free to go on as I thought best. I don't know why you put your head in the lion's mouth by asking me to find your stepdaughter – I suppose that was Simone's idea?'

No answer.

'Well, although it was wrong of you to kill her, she did unwittingly dish you by making that suggestion. And you were so furious you strangled her – probably without actually meaning to kill her – and then you attacked her corpse because her death only made matters worse.'

'What the hell are you talking about? All right, I did kill her. I killed her in a rage. But it was simply because she was unfaithful to me. So spare me your idiotic stories and be good enough to hand me over to the police!'

He wasn't lost for it.

'Right,' I said. 'Your mistress cheated on you, you saw red, and before you knew where you were you'd strangled her, then battered her round the head to teach her a lesson. So far so good. But what about the keys?' I produced them. 'How do you explain that Lecanut had the keys to this house, which he lost while he was performing his tricks on the scenic railway? And how do you account for the fact that Lecanut's suitcase is in a cupboard in there in the bedroom?'

Silence. Then: 'For the simple reason that it was with Lecanut that Simone betrayed me.'

'You're a man after my own heart! An answer for almost everything! Let's hope it lasts . . . Why did you have to use a disguise to come here at night to dig your victim's grave?'

'I'm Roussel here, not Montolieu. I've always hated making my private life public.'

'Not a very satisfactory answer.'

'Maybe not. But you'll just have to put up with it.'

I didn't answer. I stood up and took out my gun again. I thought I might have heard a noise somewhere . . .

Then the door opened and a figure appeared in the doorway.

This was why the wine merchant had come in disguise. He was expecting someone he didn't want to recognize him.

I threatened the newcomer with my revolver and told him to put his hands up. He obeyed.

He was a plump, well-dressed man of forty, with a hooked nose, rings on nearly all his fingers and a tie-pin worth a whole shirt factory in itself. He was clearly surprised to see the gun, but I wouldn't have said he was upset. I had a shrewd idea of how he made a living.

'Come in,' I told him. 'No entrance fee.'

I waved him to the other side of the room and kicked the door shut.

'This is a nice sort of reception,' the latest arrival said to Montolieu, who now looked more downcast than before. What did this mean?

'Never mind that,' I told him. 'It's a stick-up. Have you got the dough?'

'What dough?'

I looked him over. 'No, you can't have it. You'd need at least an attaché case to carry it. You're very careful, aren't you?'

'So careful I walked right into your parlour! Don't be ridiculous, monsieur . . . I'm just a peaceful citizen out for a walk . . . a solitary stroller . . .'

'Like Jean-Jacques Rousseau?'

'Yes, except that I don't like kicks up the backside.'

'Solitary stroller, my foot! Gold trafficker or fence, more like! Turn round, please . . .'

I fished the gun out from under his arm and then felt over the rest of him. He complained that I was tickling him, then suddenly lowered one arm, gripped my neck as in a vice, and gave a squirm that nearly lifted me off my feet. I could scarcely breathe. As I gasped for air I sensed that a third person was now present. Someone then gave me the traditional whack on the back of the head, and bells began to play what sounded like the Harry Lime theme.

I didn't lose consciousness completely, but I was helpless. Vague shapes moved around me: I saw them through a red haze. I felt someone searching me, then tying up my wrists and ankles, and I learned that someone who didn't like kicks up the backside didn't mind administering them. Then I was yanked up and dumped in an armchair. A slap round the face only helped to clear my head, except for a slight ache. I could soon see and hear as well as ever.

My three captors were standing in front of me: Montolieu, his hands and feet now untied; the bloke with the rings; and the newcomer who'd nearly knocked me out. This last had a thin pale face, as flat and inexpressive as a pancake except for a mean mouth. A wizard at poker, no doubt. At present he had a gun in his hand. So had the one with the rings, but he had my papers too.

'A private detective, I see,' he remarked evenly. 'How does he come into all this?'

'I'll explain later,' said Montolieu. 'It would take too long now.'

'He can explain for himself right away. He's not gagged.'

I told them how much I appreciated this favour.

The one with the rings shrugged. 'The neighbours are too far away to hear if you yell. But in any case I advise against it . . .'

Here he waggled his gun threateningly. His vampire friend followed suit.

'I shan't yell,' said I. 'I'm a big boy now. As for explaining what I'm doing here, the other gentleman is quite right . . . It would take too long.'

'I see. No one wants to talk, eh?' He turned to Montolieu angrily. 'I come here in good faith—'

'Give it a rest!' said the other. 'Good faith, indeed! You haven't even brought anything on account.'

'That's because I'm careful, as our friend the cop here says. And with reason. Midnight rendezvous in lonely surburban villas can be full of surprises. As we see. That's why Félix and I didn't come together.' Félix must be the pale one. 'You never know when a rearguard may come in useful. As for bringing something on account . . . I don't seem to see many bars of gold around.'

'Because they're not here,' said I. 'They're at Bercy. In some disused wagon tankers.'

'Shut up, you!' said Montolieu.

Félix was getting impatient. 'How much longer is this farce going on, Monsieur Raymond? I don't like the look of things.'

'Nor do I,' said Monsieur Raymond.

'You ought to go and have a peek in the bathroom,' I suggested.

'Why?'

'You might like that better. On the other hand—'

'Listen,' Montolieu interrupted, 'don't take any notice of this fellow. He's only trying to confuse us. And there are millions at stake, dammit! For you as well as for me. We ought just to talk it all over quietly.'

And he went to the sideboard and brought some glasses and the bottle of wine over to the table. When he'd served the other two, they sat looking at their glasses as if they were full of poison.

'What *is* in the bathroom?' Raymond asked me.

'The body of a woman.'

He wasn't calm now. 'What!'

And again, turning to Montolieu: 'What?'

Montolieu took a nervous swig of wine. 'My mistress,' he said.

'That beats all!' exclaimed Raymond. 'Where *is* the bathroom?'

I pointed. He made off. Montolieu poured himself some more wine. Félix, still holding his gun, still impassive and motionless, said nothing. I fidgeted a bit with my bonds, but quietly, because of the silence. Raymond reappeared.

'I don't like this at all,' said he.

'Neither do I,' Montolieu answered, 'but for heaven's sake! The girl and the cop haven't got anything to do with our business! They shouldn't prevent us from discussing it and coming to an agreement. Good grief! There are millions at stake – you're not going to let a corpse and a private eye frighten you, are you?'

'A corpse doesn't frighten me,' said Raymond. 'I've had to deal with two or three already in the course of my career. Perhaps more. But they were corpses I knew all about. Whereas this dame . . . and this witness . . .'

'We can easily bump him off too. It's a matter of millions . . .'

'Yeah . . .' Raymond stroked his chin. His rings glittered. 'You're right.' He smiled. 'Let's talk . . . After all, it *is* a matter of millions. But in view of the special circumstances I'm going to have to increase my figure. The risks are much greater than—'

'I don't see how.'

'Let's talk it over.'

They sat around the table. They made an interesting picture. Montolieu did justice to the wine. The others still didn't touch their glasses. Their heads bent closer together. They were deep in discussion. I hoped it would go on for some time. I'd managed to loosen the cord round my wrists, but there was still some way to go.

And then the door opened yet again.

Raymond and Félix whirled round in their chairs, their automatics trained on the intruder.

This was none other than a scraggy scarecrow in a *belle-époque* hat and horn-rimmed glasses. Mme Parmentier!

She keeled over like a skittle, her specs flying.

In the ensuing confusion I jumped to my still-tied-up feet, shuffled over to the table as in a sack race, grabbed hold of the bottle and hit out at the nearest head. It happened to be Raymond's. He dropped his gun. I dived down, picked it up, seized a leg of the table, and overturned it to form a shield. There was a loud bang, and something struck against the wood: Montolieu, missing me with my own gun, at a guess. Raymond was on his feet again, swearing like a trooper, rushing over to Montolieu, and telling him not to be a fool. But Montolieu was beside himself; out of all control. He must have realized the game was up: such a lot of incomprehensible things were happening, and maybe he'd had a couple of drinks too many. He now aimed his gun at Raymond, and Félix was obliged to protect his boss. He was an expert shot, and hit Montolieu in the hand, sending his gun crashing to the floor.

Montolieu followed. Raymond and Félix fell upon him, and it was then that the door . . .

No, it didn't open. It had been open ever since Mme Parmentier appeared, so the new arrivals had only to walk in, stepping round the old lady's recumbent form – except for one, who tripped over her. Inspector Grégoire stood there beside me, on the other side of the upturned table.

'Well, Burma,' said he. 'Perhaps you're pleased to see me this time?'

16 The Dregs

Two days later I went to see Mme Parmentier in the boulevard Poniatowski. It was the least I could do.

'You saved my life!' I told her. 'If you hadn't turned up and scared the crooks out of their wits—'

'Am I such a fright as all that?' she said with a smile.

'You know what I mean! They couldn't make out what was happening – especially Montolieu, who was nearly at the end of his tether already – and if you hadn't come on the scene I don't know what would have become of me. It's true the police were hovering around, because, although I didn't know it, Inspector Grégoire was having me followed. But they might have been too late. Whereas you . . . ! I hope you're all right again now – it must have been quite a shock!'

'It was indeed. As soon as I opened the door and saw those men with their guns – well, you saw! I just swooned away. I'm going to stick to fiction in future! But that conversation we had when you came to see me got me so excited I decided I must go and see what was happening in my very own house. I knew the middle of the night was the time when these things are supposed to happen, but as it rained the night after you came, I stayed at home. But the next night . . . It *was* wonderful, wasn't it?'

'Not for everybody. The two gold traffickers will be in gaol for a good long time. And, as you may have seen in the papers, your former tenant is dead. Though Félix aimed only at his hand, the bullet also hit a vital organ. And before he died, Montolieu made enough of a confession to confirm my theory about him.'

The old lady's eyes sparkled. 'I hope you've come to unveil the mystery! You did promise! Let's sit down and make ourselves comfortable. I bought some whisky especially for you . . .'

The maid brought the bottle. My hostess lit a cigarette and gave me permission to light my pipe.

'I'm breaking in a new one,' I said. 'It came through the post this morning. From Nice. A present from an unknown female admirer. Look!'

The bowl was shaped like the head of a bull, with a little spring to make it open and shut. The old lady couldn't have cared less about my female admirers. What she wanted was the story.

'It all came to me in a flash the night I persuaded Christine to go back home. Just after I left her. Her name, her fear of her stepfather, the way she walked, her mysterious reference to what she was going to do in five weeks' time when she came of age . . . She was talking about taking over her father's business – as she confirmed the next day.'

'What do you mean, "her name"?'

'Delay. I suddenly remembered that was the name on the tanker wagons in the press photographs taken at the scene of the gold robbery!'

'And what about the way she walked?'

'Well, it was just like the way Geneviève Lissert used to walk before her accident – I'd seen that in a home movie. And not only that, but Chris had auburn hair – and Gigi's hair used to be auburn too. And another thing. At first I'd thought Chris's feeling about her stepfather might be based on something improper about his attitude towards her, but now I realized it was something different. She was extremely sensitive, and had an intuition that he might do her harm. Well, all this eventually added up to a hypothesis: Montolieu, whose own "reign" was due to end in five weeks' time, might plan, and might have planned in the past, to get rid of the girl who was due to succeed him. Mightn't she have an "accident"? Hadn't he even made an attempt to carry out this plan a year ago? Montolieu knew Lecanut, and we had only his word for it that they hadn't met for years. Lecanut seemed very familiar with scenic railways. Mightn't it have been in mistake for Chris that he threw Gigi off it? It happened at night. Both girls liked to dress in the latest fashion. And in a crowd you can easily lose sight for a moment of a person you're looking for, and then take somebody else for them.'

'Just a minute,' said Mme Parmentier. She didn't read detective stories for nothing. 'Suppose there really was an earlier attempt on Christine's life? If so, why didn't the would-be murderer try again? But she seems to have been quite hale and hearty still when you last saw her – the night you took her back home! Not every attempt could have failed!'

'Quite right! It follows that there weren't any further attempts. Perhaps Montolieu took fright. Perhaps he thought his wife, who loved her daughter very much, would suspect something if Chris had a fatal "accident". But why should Montolieu want to get rid of his stepdaughter at all? She was going to inherit the business, but up till quite recently, when she began to understand the hatred she saw in his eyes, she didn't intend to turn her stepfather out . . . But wait! Even if Montolieu gave up the idea of killing her, he was still going to have to let her see the accounts. And, as he admitted before he died, he was a gambler as well as a womanizer, and had helped himself to some of the company's cash. So what was he to do to cover it up?

'Lecanut was mixed up in the gold robbery. The raid took place near some tankers belonging to Delay and Montolieu. Was Montolieu involved? Was the robbery his way of trying to square the Bercy accounts? Were the two or three ingots found on the beach at Palavas a mere red herring, and was the main haul hidden in one of the tankers?'

'And was it?'

I pulled a face. 'The other night at Saint-Mandé, before the gold traffickers arrived, I thought the tankers in the press photos of the robbery were now at Bercy, and that the famous reward was as good as mine. But I was wrong. Faroux sent his chaps to Bercy to investigate. The tankers there *were* the ones that had been near the scene of the robbery, and they'd even been used to transport the swag, but—'

'They're empty!' cried Mme Parmentier.

'Precisely. And Montolieu died without saying where the present hiding-place is.'

'Too bad,' said the old bird. 'But that doesn't stop you from telling me the rest of your theory.'

The reward meant nothing to her. She had a private income.

'The very day after I formed my theory I had to revise it. I'd told Montolieu not to tell the police he knew Lecanut just so that I'd have a witness up my sleeve – at that point I didn't suspect him of anything. But when Faroux told me Montolieu had gone and volunteered information, I realize he must have been deliberately trying to put a spoke in my wheel . . . But why? . . . Then there was the matter of Simone and her taxi ride. I couldn't get hold of the cab driver, but another detective story addict promised to get hold of him for me. These thriller addicts are worth their weight in gold, as you have amply proved, my dear lady!'

Mme Parmentier preened herself.

'But I couldn't get hold of Simone. For the very good reason that while I was chatting with Christine in my car, Simone was getting herself bumped off. I'd gone to see Christine to make sure what she meant about ruling the roost. The same day I saw the disused tankers at Bercy. I was more and more convinced that my theory was right. But how was I to explode my bombshell? I didn't want to go to Faroux – I prefer to work on my own. (And there was no particular hurry, except to get Chris out of Paris. I'm fond of the kid, and I didn't want her to get caught in the fall-out. Anyhow, I persuaded her to go away in the end . . .) Well, the taxi driver eventually showed me where he'd picked Simone up. I got into your house by using the keys Lecanut dropped. And there I found the body.'

'Did you know who the murderer was straight away?'

'I don't really know. Anyway, I wasn't surprised when I eventually recognized Montolieu underneath the disguise. But at the time I discovered the corpse I didn't bother my head too much about the killer – the case was all over bar the shouting: all I had to do was set up a trap in your villa. In that connection I made enquiries about your tenant. Not that it got me very far. Except, of course, for meeting you – that turned out to be *very* useful!'

'Only too pleased!' cooed Mme Parmentier.

I relit my pipe and went on. 'Here's a recap of the plot, rounded out by Montolieu's deathbed confession. After Delay's death, Montolieu became the boss of the wine business, and was due to remain so until Christine came of age. Three years ago he married Marthe, Delay's widow, who'd already been his mistress while Delay was still alive. Apparently he only married her out of self-interest, to strengthen his position in the business: he had various other liaisons by now. He also helped himself from the till. Lecanut had left the firm, but the two men were still in touch, and last year, when Montolieu decided to get rid of Christine, he turned to his former colleague – whom, by the way, the police suspect of having been a specialist in fairground "accidents". Lecanut duly turned up, and to plan the crime the two men met in your villa, which Montolieu had rented under the name of Roussel, to use as a love-nest, if you'll forgive the expression. But Lecanut botched the job and threw the wrong girl off the switchback. His excuse was that he hadn't seen Christine for such a long time. Montolieu then gave up the idea of killing her, but he still had to make good the gaps in the accounts. What about a robbery? Not so serious as murder, he thought (the killing of the two guards at Montpellier wasn't part of the original plan). Montolieu knew someone who worked for the Precious Metals Consortium, and who tipped him the wink about a gold consignment that would be hanging about for a few days at Montpellier. He called Lecanut in again. Montolieu sent some tankers down; Lecanut arranged the actual theft, recruiting Troyenny, the fire-eater, and another accomplice whose name Montolieu claimed not to know and who died later, according to Lecanut. The raid took place, the guards were shot, the thieves got away with part of the gold, and stashed it in the tanker. Then—'

'Hold on a minute, please,' said Mme Parmentier. 'I gather you don't think Troyenny ever knew where the gold was hidden, even though he did take part in the robbery . . .'

'Yes – with rather too much enthusiasm! Lecanut had to tell him to beat it as fast as possible after the guards were killed. So he didn't see what became of the stolen ingots. Well, once the deed was done, all the thieves had to do was wait for things to cool down, and then turn the gold into money and divide up the spoils. But this had to happen before Christine came of age. Meanwhile, Montolieu went on helping himself to cash from the company till, in order to subsidize his hidden accomplices. This he did through Lecanut, now known as Lancelin. Then the day of reckoning approached. Lecanut had found some possible purchasers for the gold, appointments had been made, and so on. Lecanut came to Paris, where he was to stay at your villa with "Roussel" and Simone – Montolieu's mistress and a party to the plot. She must have known Lecanut, too, but Montolieu didn't have time to explain about that before he died. But by the time Lecanut arrived, Montolieu's stepdaughter had disappeared, and he was afraid she or her mother might do something foolish. At this juncture he didn't dare go to the police. And his nervousness communicated itself to Lecanut, who was already on edge because of the two policemen he thought were taking an interest in him at the Gare de Lyon. So he didn't tell Montolieu who the prospective purchasers of the gold were.'

'And then?'

'Then Montolieu went home, handing over the keys of your villa to Lecanut. He and Simone stayed together and went to the Foire du Trône, where perhaps Lecanut meant to warn Troyenny that the day of reckoning was nigh. At Nation he spotted me, imagined something was up, and decided to eliminate me. He took the risk of getting Simone to lead me on and lure me on to the scenic railway—'

'Why the scenic railway?' objected my hostess. 'If Simone hooked you she could just have led you to some dark corner, and—'

'Yes, but that would have been outright murder, whereas on the scenic railway it would look like an accident. And even if I wasn't killed, I'd be out of action for a while. Like Geneviève Lissert. But, as you know, the plan didn't come off. And Simone, although she was so cool later on, fainted.'

'Or pretended to.'

'No, I think it was genuine. But I was a bit suspicious anyway, and went round to see her next day. There didn't seem to be anything amiss, but as soon as I'd gone she must have phoned Montolieu at Bercy. Then they met in the villa at Saint-Mandé for a council of war. He didn't tell her what he knew about me, but they decided to keep a watch on me between the two of them: Simone would go on giving me the glad eye, and Montolieu, at her suggestion, would call me in to trace his stepdaughter. So Simone gave me a friendly reception the next time I showed up in the rue de la Brèche-aux-Loups, lulling my suspicions until the fight at the Fair awakened them again. In fact, Simone had nothing to do with that incident, but the fact was that the two of them were out of luck.

'When I found Montolieu's daughter even before he asked me to look for her, he seems to have thought he smelled a rat. Everything seemed to be going wrong. He had the gold, but didn't know what to do with it, or who the alleged purchasers were, or where. He flung out of his house in a rage and went to the villa, where he had a row with Simone – perhaps over her suggestion about me – and accidentally killed her.

'That didn't help. He tried to get me off his back by going to the police. All he could do now was wait to find out about the purchasers, filling in the time by digging a grave. He didn't know there was anything to lead me from Simone to him – she hadn't told him about the taxi incident – and of course he had no idea I had Lecanut's keys. Then one night, the night it rained, he had an idea, and came and ripped up

Lecanut's case. In the lining he found the names and addresses of the prospective purchasers of the gold, who must be wondering if they were ever going to see the vendor: they knew Lecanut as Lancelin, so the incident at the Foire du Trône didn't mean anything to them – they didn't know he was dead. Next day Montolieu went to see them, using the name Roussel, and arranged to meet them at the villa. The rest you know.'

Mme Parmentier lit her umpteenth Gauloise. I had another Scotch. Then I got up to leave. My hostess saw me out.

'I suppose you might call it a tragedy of errors,' she said, breathing smoke out through her nostrils like a little old dragon. 'Everybody concerned made mistakes. Lecanut last year, when he attacked Mlle Lissert, and again the other night, when he tried to kill you. Troyenny, by going to your place. Simone, by trying to cover up about the taxi and by advising Montolieu to call you in to find Christine. Montolieu himself by taking her advice, and then going on to make things worse. Inspector Grégoire, at the very beginning, by thinking you knew Lancelin . . .'

'That's right. No need to go on,' I said. 'Everyone made mistakes. Except me. As usual.'

'Come, come – you made at least one.'

'You mean about the tanker?'

'No – that was only half a mistake. Your real error' – she smiled – 'was to think that if you merely mentioned M. Delay's death in passing, that would satisfy me and stop me from drawing my own conclusions.'

Grandmamma, what big eyes you've got! thought I.

Nothing escapes them. If she'd been fifty years younger I'd have offered her a job on the spot.

I laughed. 'You read too many detective stories,' I told her.

'Luckily for you,' she retorted. 'Anyhow, come back and see me some time.'

She gave a wink, meaning 'when you decide to tell me everything'.

At least, that's what I hope she meant.

I got back into the car. I'd speechified to Mme Parmentier, but I wasn't going to go and boast of my prowess to ex-Mme Montolieu, formerly ex-Mme Delay: she had enough troubles already. Things must take their course. The police would probably find out, but not through me. I hadn't had to wait for the old lady's hint to realize that Delay had been pushed into that wine-vat of his. I'd known as soon as I heard about the so-called accident. His wife had got fed up with him and consoled herself with his partner, who once the pair of them had got Delay out of the way turned out to be just as unsatisfactory a husband as his predecessor. Poor Marthe! she'd had to endure her second marriage as a kind of expiation, concentrating all her love on her daughter. If you asked me, Montolieu was lucky Lecanut made a mess of murdering his stepdaughter – it was only Chris's presence that stopped Marthe from giving him away about Delay. That was why he got so uptight when she disappeared – in case Marthe got distraught, imagined he was behind it, and did something rash. Another reason for calling me in, though he soon regretted it. He was like all criminals

– too cool one minute and not cool enough the next. Sharp as you like one day, dim as hell another. Take that idea of digging Simone's grave in the most difficult place he could find . . .

I'd refrained from swearing at Mme Parmentier's. Now the oaths poured forth like a firework display. I stopped the car and hared to the nearest phone.

'Faroux?' I gasped. 'The bars of gold!'

'Have you found them?'

'Yes. They're buried in the garden of the villa at Saint-Mandé!'

'You think so? I had my men dig it over, and I'm not so sure.'

'They're there all right. Montolieu wouldn't have started digging Simone's grave in the stoniest part of the garden if there hadn't been something in the less stony parts that he didn't want to disturb.'

That was three days ago.

They did find the hundred and fifty kilos of gold under the lawn. And I've just collected the famous reward. It's here in my breast pocket. An oblong piece of pink paper that's like a weight on my heart.

The great station clock is bending its horrible eye on me once more. As if the story were starting all over again. But some things never start again . . .

This time Hélène really *is* arriving at the Gare de Lyon. And last week a girl, pretty, sensitive and full of life, left from there on the Mistral, more or less because of me.

That was my real mistake, Mme Parmentier! Trying to get Chris away from the fall-out from the bomb I was about to explode. What a hope! The cops pressed their investigations so far that Marthe Montolieu confessed to her part in her husband's murder. And her daughter found out about it down there in the south, all alone. And she was so sensitive. Too sensitive. If she'd still been here I might have been able to protect her from herself.

As it was, just as I left the office where those solemn gentlemen, all dressed up, had handed me the reward, together with their thanks and congratulations, I bought a copy of the *Crépuscule* and learned that she had committed suicide.

Paris, 1957